HOLIDAY SHIFTERS
CLEAN PARANORMAL HOLIDAY ROMANCE

NORTH POLE UNIVERSITY
BOOK ONE

MARIE-HÉLÈNE LEBEAULT

BEACHES AND TRAILS
PUBLISHING

1

KAYLA

Christmas used to be my favourite time of year. As you grow older, it loses some of its magic. It's hard to maintain the eager anticipation of youth when you send your parents an Amazon Wishlist. Don't get me wrong, I love Christmas; it's still the Most Wonderful Time of the Year. However, when you're sixteen, and the only plans you have for the winter break are mandatory reading and work, it takes away some of the sparkle and shine of Christmas.

"Ingrid, can I leave an hour early today? I still have a few more presents to buy," I pleaded with my manager.

Mum and Dad were so proud when I told them I got a job at *La Patisserie* just outside London. We'd argued a lot about my first job. They thought it would give me independence and teach me how the world works. I thought that it would be yet another demand on my time, but I loved it once I started.

The small, family-owned bakery had a total of six employees, including me. Claude, the baker, his wife Pauline, and their daughters Marion and Penelope. The latter was my age and great fun to work with. And there was Ingrid, the Polish manager they had hired to help promote and run the bakery. She ran a tight ship, but I was confident she would agree to my request. It was four p.m. on Christmas Eve, and the shop was empty not only of customers, but of wares to sell. They had completely wiped us out. Claude and his family were prepping for the next day, and I had finished tallying the sales and tidying up the small café area.

Ingrid glanced over at Claude. The Frenchman smiled and winked at me. "Sure, go ahead, and Happy Christmas," Ingrid said with a smile.

I jumped with glee, clapping my hands excitedly. "Thank you, thank you, thank you!" I beamed, flinging my arms around the manager in a tight hug. I could tell it was making her uncomfortable, so I stepped back and said, "Happy Christmas, Ingrid!"

I pulled my apron off and ran to the back to hug Claude and his family. "Joyeux Noël!" I told them on my way to the staff room to grab my things.

Wrapping my coat tightly around myself, I pulled on my grey wool hat, matching scarf, and gloves. It had to be -5 outside. Winter this year had been exceptionally bitter; I couldn't remember it ever being quite so cold.

I flung on my backpack and headed out before Claude caught up with me.

"Attend," he said, handing me a small white cardboard box wrapped in brown twine. A small white envelope was tucked inside. It was stamped with a gold snowflake, and my name was written in gold ink in the most beautiful calligraphy I had ever seen.

"Happy Christmas," he said with a thick accent. "Some Christmas goodies for you and your family and a Christmas bonus for all your hard work these last few months."

I thanked him and opened the envelope, curious to see what was inside. There was a hundred-pound note in it! "Oh my gosh, Claude. It's too much! I promise I'll come in early for my next shift," I said, barely suppressing the tears that welled in my eyes. This man and his family had already done so much for me.

"*Ne t'inquiète pas, petite,*" he replied, waiving away my objections.

My French had significantly improved at the Patisserie, so I replied, "*Merci beaucoup, Claude. Joyeux Noël,*" as I blew a kiss and headed for the next train into London.

Another thing that took some of the magic away from Christmas was trying to navigate the London Underground. London was busy enough any other time of the year, but it seemed even more chaotic at Christmas. Tourists from all over the world come to spend the holiday season here; the bright lights and the big city drew people like moths to a flame. Pushing past everyone, I headed up the stairs from the Underground towards my favourite place to shop in London: Oxford Street.

London at Christmas was breathtaking. Every storefront, every tree was bathed in light. But the place that really made my heart sing was Oxford Street. I took in the display. A huge Christmas angel was suspended between the storefronts on either side of the street; its wings spread wide as if in flight. It always amazed me how they managed to make an angel out of lights look so lifelike. The cold air whipped at my face, but I couldn't move; I couldn't tear my gaze away from the Christmas angel. My skin was covered in goosebumps, and I shivered from delight as well as the cold. This was the true magic of Christmas.

For just a moment, I swore the angel's wings actually moved, and a strange tingling sensation ran through my body. It felt like the air was charged with something I couldn't name but somehow recognized deep within. I dismissed it as excitement, but part of me wondered if there was something more to the feeling.

CONNOR

Tonight was the night. I was finally going to get my shot. A week before last Christmas, I travelled to the North Pole to participate in the reindeer games: three days of tryouts to test character, agility, magic control, and spirit.

Being part of the team that pulled Santa's sleigh on Christmas Eve was a true honour for my family. And yes, I'm talking about the real Santa, not some fake, storefront set-up.

I first shifted into my reindeer form two years ago when I was fifteen, and ever since, I had dreamed of being a part of Santa's team.

My family hadn't had a place on the team since my great, great, great grandfather. Santa had lost his trust in the Prancer family after my grandfather arrived late one Christmas Eve. He was supposed to lead the other reindeer, and he wasn't just a little late either. He had overslept and arrived almost three hours late. Santa demoted him to the third spot and moved Jacob Rudolph to the front of the herd.

Everyone knows the story of Rudolph, the famous, red-nosed

reindeer. For generations, the Rudolph family rode his wave of fame until Sarah Blitzen won the reindeer games and was granted the lead of the herd.

It was my family's turn. Unfortunately, we have a bit of a reputation for being foul-tempered. When Jacob Rudolph was promoted above my grandfather, the winner of the reindeer games, he lost his temper and almost ruined Christmas. Santa's a great guy, but it took him a long time to trust anyone from my family again.

My parents had hoped I might be accepted to North Pole University, where many shifters trained in magical arts and holiday traditions. It was the most prestigious education a young shifter could receive, but I'd need to prove myself first. The first full moon after my fifteenth birthday, I turned. The very next day, I cracked open the reindeer shifter history books.

I practised every full moon and did everything I possibly could to hone my skills. I wanted to be a part of the team so badly. I needed everyone to see that my family had honour and integrity. Despite our bad tempers, we were good people and great reindeer.

Reindeer shifters worldwide make the trip to the North Pole every December for the reindeer games. Shifters who live in frigid climes tend to win because they are used to the frosty conditions. Hundreds take part, and each year, only nine are chosen. I was one of them this year. Not just one of them, I had been granted the lead position. I was so excited that I felt like I had eaten one hundred sugar pops and was on a permanent sugar high. I could already feel Santa's magic running through my veins. Mum even said that I was walking a little taller; it truly was a dream come true. For all of us Prancers.

The tradition was that the chosen shifters would take their family's portal to the North Pole at eight o'clock on Christmas Eve. We would have dinner with Santa and go over the plans for the evening. We would discuss the route to take, the speeds, commands, and safety. And, at midnight when the moon was at its highest, we would shift to our reindeer forms, gear up, and fly.

I wanted to show Santa that he had chosen the right reindeer for the job. His trust in me was something I treasured. I wouldn't repeat the mistakes of the past, and I took my responsibility seriously.

I needed an outfit for dinner that said, 'Santa, I won't disappoint you.' It also had to say, 'I'm a Rockstar,' because that's exactly how I felt.

I usually hated shopping. I let my sister do it for me; she's so much better at it. But tonight was different; I needed just the right ensemble to fit the occasion.

I had spent the better part of three hours going from store to store, but nothing seemed to fit what I had in mind. I wanted something more in tune with Christmas, something festive and fun.

This is hopeless, I thought to myself after leaving another store empty-handed.

I watched as everyone hurried around the well-lit streets while Christmas carols boomed from the loudspeakers. It gave me chills, but the good kind. I enjoyed people watching, seeing everyday people go about their lives, unaware of all the magic surrounding them. I always wondered how different things would be if people didn't lose their belief in magic as they grew up.

It was one of the best things about being a shifter, seeing and feeling the magic in everything around me. I turned and headed up towards Oxford Street, hoping to find what I was looking for.

I sighed as I admired the Christmas decorations – the snowflakes, the flashing Santas, and even the glittering reindeer, which made me laugh. Each store looked like they were trying to outdo the store before on levels of Christmas spirit.

The air was electric; it made me even more excited for midnight. I was so lost in the moment that I didn't pay attention to where I was going. I walked straight into a girl. She had apparently decided that the middle of the street was the perfect place to stand and stare into space.

"Sorry," I said simply, grabbing her shoulders so we wouldn't tumble to the ground. She barely registered what had happened, so I kept going. I felt a pull towards Jessie's, a department store. I could feel the magic pulling me inside; my outfit called to me. I could feel it.

2

KAYLA

"Would you like that gift wrapped, miss?" asked the sales clerk whose name tag read Tom.

"Yes, please," I replied with a grin.

I stood waiting and breathed a sigh of relief; I had finally bought the last of my Christmas gifts, my outfit for Christmas Day, and still had a little money to spare.

"Jingle Bell Rock" played over the store speakers as I watched Tom fold the brown leather jacket I had bought for Dad and place it neatly in a large white box. I marvelled at how elegantly he folded the red wrapping paper decorated with snowflakes and finished it off with a white and silver glittering ribbon. It was impressive.

I checked my phone and saw I had two messages. The first was from my Mum reminding me that dinner was at eight-thirty and to message her as soon as I was on the train home. The second text was from my BFF, Louise. She had sent pictures of the dress and shoes she bought for a New Year's Eve party and was panicked because she couldn't find a bag to match. Little did she know, I had the perfect bag for her as her gift.

"Here you go, have a Happy Christmas," Tom said, handing me the large bag containing all my gifts.

"Thanks, you too!" I smiled back and headed downstairs. My shoulders ached from carrying the multiple bags. I looked out of the large windows on the second floor and noticed it had started to snow. I hated the cold, that feeling of not being able to move your fingers as the freezing temperatures froze your joints.

I checked the time and saw that I still had about an hour before the store closed and about an hour and a half before I had to catch the last train to Kent.

The idea of waiting in the cold London Underground held no appeal, so I headed to Jessie's famous café next to the home department. As I approached the café, the smell of gingerbread, chocolate, and coffee filled the air. It wrapped around me like a blanket. I inhaled deeply, not wanting to miss any of the fragrances.

The café was still busy; five people were ahead of me in line, but I didn't mind. I needed time to decide on what I wanted. Glancing at the Christmas specials, mint chocolate mocha jumped out at me.

"Yep, that's what I'm having," I said out loud rather cheerfully, forgetting I was standing in a busy café.

The couple in front of me turned and gave me a look like I was a crazy person. I could feel my cheeks go red with embarrassment.

"Sounds good. What was your choice again?" asked a smooth, friendly voice I didn't recognise. Confused, I turned around and saw the cutest guy I had ever seen in my life. He looked like something out of the pages of a magazine: tall, with short dark hair, green eyes, and a chiselled jawline to rival George Clooney's.

"Wow," I breathed.

He chuckled and his face lit up like a Christmas tree. He was amazing! My stomach knotted in excitement, butterflies fluttering around, making me shift uneasily from foot to foot.

"I'm in the mood to celebrate, and I hate to drink alone. Can I buy you a coffee?" he asked.

How romantic, straight out of a romcom! Did I want a cute guy to buy me a coffee? DUH!

"That would be brilliant," I replied though I had meant not to sound quite so eager. He smiled and asked, "What are you having?"

When I told him, he chuckled once more and replied, "Excellent choice. I think I will have the same."

I couldn't believe a guy like him was talking to me. I'm not one to toot my own horn; I'm pretty enough. But the kind of girl that random guys flirt with? My friend Louise was such a girl. I'm short for my age, with cropped brown hair, a button nose, and eyes too big for my face. It gives me a slightly cartoonish look that most people would describe as cute.

When we were about to sit down at one of the café tables, his phone buzzed. He checked it, and when he looked up, joy and elation seemed to leech out of his face. What appeared next were shock, worry, and regret. He was so expressive.

"I'm so sorry, but I have someplace I need to be," and before I knew it, he was gone.

CONNOR

I was running dangerously late. One thing about being one of Santa's reindeer is that the magic running through you on Christmas Eve is stronger. Shifters usually turn on the full moon. As it was Christmas Eve and a full moon, my body was pulsing like a disco ball. I needed to be somewhere safe when night came because I was only just learning to control my shifting.

I made a beeline for the elevators only to come face-to-face with an out-of-order sign. It directed customers to the lifts in the toy department. Navigating the toy department would be like running an obstacle course, so I decided taking the stairs would be a wiser course of action.

As luck would have it, the door to the stairs was locked, and a similar sign was posted on the door. The toy department it was going to be then.

I pushed my way through the crowds and was happy to see no sign by the elevator doors and, more importantly, no one else waiting.

"Finally," I said with relief as the double doors opened with the electronic ping. I ran inside, lodging myself in the corner. I closed my eyes and started to sing along with the song that was playing in the elevator. It was "Silent Night," and it was soothing. As I sang, I began to relax, and the urge to shift slowly receded. Breathe in, breathe out.

"Hold the doors, please," yelled a voice that sounded oddly familiar. My eyes flew open, and, on instinct, I stuck out my hand to stop the doors from closing. Why had I done that? I needed to get out of here as fast as possible.

"Thank you so much," said the voice as the girl from the café stepped inside, struggling with the multitude of bags she carried. She took one look at me and muttered, "Oh, it's you."

The cheery girl was gone. The one that stood before me was cold and angry. I couldn't blame her. I'd flirted with her, bought her a cup of coffee, and bolted before I could even ask her name.

Her large blue eyes, the colour of a moonless night at the North Pole, looked back at me blankly. Those plush lips that shone as the light reflected off her pink lip gloss were pursed in a disapproving pout.

I smiled awkwardly, casting my eyes everywhere around the elevator to avoid making eye contact. She stood in the opposite corner, facing the wall rather than the jerk that had left her hanging.

I'm not going to lie – that stung a little. If it had been any other day, I'd have jumped at the chance to get to know her.

We stood in silence as the lift sprang into action and made its way to the ground floor. *Beep* went the elevator as the numbers above the door highlighted the floor as we passed, then a loud bang. The lift stopped, the lights flickered on and off several times, and the music stopped playing.

I pushed past the girl and pressed the open button, but

nothing happened. In a panic, I pressed all the buttons, but still, nothing happened.

The gravity of the situation dawned on me all too quickly. I checked my watch; it was almost five. The sun had set, and the moon was out. If I didn't control myself, I might shift in here, with her.

I'm big in my reindeer form, bigger than most my age, and I wasn't all that friendly after going through the transition from man to animal.

In a space this small, I'd likely crush her or, at the very least, scare her to death. It was straight out of a horror movie.

I could feel the magic building in my veins—hot and cold pulses shooting through my body as my reindeer form struggled to emerge. If I shifted here, I'd not only expose our kind to a human but possibly hurt her in the process. Professor Blitzen's warnings from shifter orientation echoed in my mind: "Control is the first lesson any shifter must master."

Get a grip. Breathe in, breathe out.

But I couldn't seem to catch my breath. Was there sufficient ventilation in the lift? The space was getting smaller and smaller, the walls closing in on me.

3
KAYLA

Oh great, as if being stuck in a lift wasn't bad enough; I'm stuck in here with the vanishing boy. I thought to myself, dropping my bags.

"Calm down. You're making me nervous," I said a little more brusquely than I intended. "We just need to press the emergency button," I said more softly, opening the hatch below the controls. I pressed the emergency call button, and immediately someone asked, "Hello, how can I help?"

"We're stuck. The lift stopped between the first and the ground floor. Can you send an engineer to get us out?" I asked.

We waited a few moments before a grainy reply floated through the speakers.

"Unfortunately, as it's Christmas Eve, we do not have an engineer on-site. We will have to call one in, and the current wait time is a couple of hours. We will let you know as soon as they arrive."

"What?" the boy yelled from the far corner. His eyes seemed to glow unnaturally. Not from unshed tears, but like they were lit from the inside. *It has to be from the emergency light overhead.* I shook the thought off and put it down to the look a crazy person gets when they feel trapped.

I let out a frustrated groan, trying to ignore the annoying pacing he was doing in the space that was already small enough. I pulled my phone out of my pocket. *I better call Mum and let her know I'm running late*, I thought.

"You have got to be kidding me!" I groaned. There was no signal.

It was my turn to panic. My mind was racing with a hundred different thoughts.

What am I going to do? I can't call for help, I can't call Mum, and I can't exactly ask this guy because he needs all the help he can get.

Crossing my arms, I leaned against the wall and watched as he franticly ran his hands through his hair.

"Are you okay?" I asked, genuinely starting to worry.

"No, not really. I have to get out of here," he stammered.

"I think you're having a panic attack. Sit down and put your head between your knees," I said confidently.

I had seen enough panic attacks to know how scary they could be. He looked back at me with confusion. I swear I saw his eyes shimmer again. Maybe he was crying.

"Sit," I said firmly, pointing to the ground. Slowly, he sank to the floor and rested his head on the back of his arms. I crouched down in front of him.

"Take deep, slow breaths. In through your nose, out through your mouth," I said, my voice as soothing as I could manage.

After a few minutes, he was calmer, and his breathing returned to normal. "Thank you," he breathed, keeping his eyes closed. "That really helped."

"Don't mention it," I said and went back to my side of the elevator. I sat cross-legged, gathering my shopping bags around me like they might protect me somehow.

"I'm sorry about before. I didn't mean to be rude," he started. "I lost track of time, and I'm running really late for a work thing. And now I might lose the gig entirely," he said, finally looking at me. His eyes didn't shine, but the sadness in them was heart-breaking.

I pulled the box from *La Patisserie* out of my backpack and opened it to see shortbread cookies in assorted Christmas shapes. I handed him the cookie shaped like a reindeer.

"Here, have a cookie. It might cheer you up!" I said.

He looked at the cookie and started laughing. I couldn't help feeling a little annoyed. *Jerk.*

"I'm glad you find it so amusing. I was just being nice," I said. Before I could put the cookie back in the box, he grabbed my hand gently.

"I want the cookie. I'm sorry for laughing. It's only that I love reindeer, and that's the cookie you picked out of all the shapes in the box."

He let go of my arm and turned his hand, palm up. I put the cookie in it. And as our hands touched, I felt a shiver down my spine and goosebumps all over my body. My cheeks were burning, and when I would have looked away, I caught sight of those green eyes and was mesmerised. He took the cookie with his other hand and popped it into his mouth.

"Hi, I'm Connor," he said. His empty hand was waiting for me, hovering in the air between us. "I'm Kayla," I said, placing my hand in his.

CONNOR

Kayla. What a pretty name.

She was a beautiful girl. She calmed me down, which was surprising, considering I had a lot to worry about. She distracted me, which helped control the magic flowing within me. I could fight off the change a little longer.

We talked for what felt like hours. She told me all the gifts she had bought, taking each gift-wrapped box out and describing the contents in detail. I should have been bored to tears, but everything Kayla said was fascinating to me.

I showed her the three-piece green tartan suit, crisp white shirt, and red tie I had bought for my 'work event.' She raised an eyebrow and replied, "It will bring out your eyes."

It was small talk, but it felt like a momentous occasion. Then, the subject moved on to school, work, and family. I couldn't exactly tell her my life story. So, I told her my family ran a reindeer ranch, which was partly true; we had regular reindeer on our farm that we used for events, mainly around Christmas.

We talked about our Christmas plans. I told her my family went up North every year for a large family reunion. It was close enough to the truth. Before long, the subject moved to the magic of Christmas. When she talked about the decorations on Oxford Street, I realised that she was the girl in the street. Though she had lost a bit of her childhood innocence, I could tell it was in there lurking, wanting to believe.

We laughed and joked and ate all of her cookies. At one point, I scooted closer to look at pictures of her family and friends on her phone. I showed her mine, and she thought it was hilarious that I also had many reindeer pictures in there. I didn't mention those were also family pictures.

I was so engrossed in Kayla's company that I forgot I almost shifted right in front of her. In a way, time seemed to stand still, like the world around us had stopped just so we could share this moment. "Thanks again for before. I, well, I..." I stammered, and she giggled. It made my stomach flip.

"It's fine," she said, putting a hand on my upper arm. Our eyes locked. Her eyes were beautiful. They were big, and they gave her a doll-like appearance that was too adorable not to love. We stared into each other's eyes for what seemed like an eternity. No words passed our lips; we were communicating on the level of the soul.

I leaned in and paused, trying to gauge if she wanted the same thing I did. In response, she scooted a little closer.

"Kayla, can I ask you something?" I asked, so quietly I'm surprised she even heard me.

"Sure," she whispered back, her eyes never leaving mine.

"May I kiss you?" I asked, inching my way closer to her, ready to stop if she said no but hoping she didn't.

"Uh-huh," she hummed, her voice barely audible as she too inched closer.

I pressed my lips to hers and scooted closer still so I could cup her face in my hands. It was magical. Electric. Perfect.

4

KAYLA

My skin tingled at his touch, and the butterflies in my stomach felt like they were dancing the flamenco. I never wanted this moment to end.

Just then, the lift jolted back to life, and the spell was broken.

We both jumped up in shock. The lights flickered on, the music started playing, and before we knew it, the doors to the lobby opened wide, revealing the store still full of shoppers. I glanced at my watch; we had only been in here for forty-five minutes.

I turned to him and grinned, about to ask if we might meet up for a date after Christmas. But he pulled another disappearing act. One minute he's caressing my face, and the next, he's shooting out of the lift and yelling, "I'm sorry. I really have to go."

I just stood there watching him vanish through the crowd.

"What the snow in Christmas was that?" I said, loud enough that passers-by looked over at me before the doors closed once again. I quickly pressed the button and got out of the lift. The engineer was waiting to see if we were okay. I told him I was fine, and that the other kid had to leave.

The store manager apologised profusely and asked if there was anything they could do. As I had missed the last train, I wondered if they could send me home in a taxi. He called a cab, and I left the store with an enormous Christmas basket. Not a total loss, then.

On the ride home, my mind kept drifting back to the kiss. I'd been kissed before, but never like that. Never had I experienced the time-standing-still connection that I felt with Connor. I couldn't help feeling disappointed that I would never see him again.

"Did you have fun shopping, dear?" Mum asked as I walked in the door. Despite the ordeal in the lift, I made it home at roughly the same time as if I'd taken the train, so I didn't mention it. She would only worry. Mostly I didn't tell her because I thought I might cry if I had to explain about Connor.

I pushed the thought out of my mind and focused on the here and now: Christmas with my family. I ate, danced, and sang with Mum, Dad, and my little brother Andy. I helped Andy set up a plate of milk and cookies for Santa before he went to bed.

"Don't forget the carrots for the reindeer," Andy insisted.

After putting Andy to bed, I crawled into my own and fell asleep.

CONNOR

I ran all the way home, clutching my shopping bag and repeating Kayla's name over and over like a mantra. I must have looked like a demented teenager, but it had the benefit of clearing my path out of Oxford Street. Remembering our kiss is what kept me in human form.

When I got home, everyone was worried. I sagged against the door like I'd been chased by bandits. I was safe. The house was charmed to keep us from shifting inside – it got messy.

"We expected you back ages ago!" Mum said. She took one look at the feral look in my eye and didn't question me further when I only said, "Long story."

There was no time for a shower, so I freshened up quickly and put my new suit on.

"How do I look?" I asked as I came back to the living room.

"You look great, son," said Dad, choking up a bit as he checked my tie.

"Please don't ever wear that here in London," said my sister, eyeing the tartan suit. I smiled at the good-natured ribbing.

We had a light Christmas dinner as a family before I had to leave for the North Pole. I gave my family the G-rated version of my adventure at the department store. Everyone shared their own stories of near misses.

When it was time to go, I stood in front of the portal, aka the fireplace, and wished my family a Happy Christmas. I'd crash at Santa's after the delivery and be home after the debriefing brunch.

Dinner with Santa and the others was incredible. Not only was the food delicious, but it never seemed to end. It was like the feasts in Harry Potter. I found I had a bottomless appetite. Santa explained that we'd be working for twelve hours straight and that we'd need our strength. Though he'd be getting a steady stream of cookies and milk, all we would get were a handful of carrots to share.

When it was finally go-time, I thought I might die of excitement. I stood tall and proud at the front of the group, wearing my family's gold crest around my neck.

"Let's give the children of the world the best Christmas yet. Onward Prancer; lead the way," boomed Santa.

As Santa shook the reins, a sparkling gold mist travelled up and curled under the sleigh. The reindeer all grunted with glee, and I knew that was my cue to go. I charged forward, climbing an invisible staircase and picking up speed. Soon we were zooming through the skies. The Prancers were back, and we were here to stay.

5
KAYLA

"Kayla, Kayla, come quick, let's open presents," Andy screamed as he ran into my room, jumping on my bed with childish glee.

I gave him a tight hug and followed him downstairs. The tree was magnificent as always, fragrant and lush.

Mum took pride in decorating the tree. This year, her colour scheme was silver and blue. Baubles, snowflakes, and ribbons decorated the tree so elegantly. A large silver glass star sat proudly on top.

"Come on, Kayla, open presents with me," my brother chirped, dancing around the tree looking for gifts with his name on them. He tossed a gift to Dad, who almost didn't catch it in time. He was walking out of the kitchen and was trying not to spill his cup of coffee.

"Hold on, champ," Dad said, putting his festive mug on a side table and wrapping each of us in a hug.

Mum did the same and came to sit next to me on the couch.

Andy ran to me and said, "Look, this one is for you," he

beamed, handing me a small red box wrapped in green tartan ribbon. I pulled the ribbon and opened the box. When I saw what was inside, every inch of my body prickled with goosebumps.

Inside sat a reindeer-shaped cookie with a gold ribbon tied around its neck and a small card.

Merry Christmas, Kayla.
Call me tomorrow.
Connor xo
0203 978 5555

6

KAYLA

Despite the cold of the snowy Boxing Day weather, I sat on the swing that Dad had built for Andy in our backyard. To my surprise, I wasn't cold; adrenaline pumped through my veins as I stared down at the card I had found under the Christmas tree.

How did it get under the tree? Should I call? I asked myself as I swung back and forth.

Part of me worried that it was a mean practical joke, but I had told no one about Connor. Any normal person would be scared, and if I told Louise about this, I could guarantee her response would be "Stalker!" If I decided to call Connor, I wanted to keep us a secret until I knew he would stick around because, let's face it, he has a track record for bolting.

The green tartan wrapping had me thinking of the suit he showed me in the lift. I wondered how he looked in it. Did the green bring out his eyes as I had thought it would? Those eyes. They had flashed and glowed when we were trapped in the lift together. I mulled over our conversation; he had been vague about much of his life, and I had just skipped past the strangeness of his glowing, amazing eyes. Did he have a secret? Did I want to find out?

A slight breeze brushed over me, making my skin prickle in the cold, and I swear the writing glowed a little brighter in my hand. I could still feel Connor's kiss on my lips. A part of me wanted to see him again and learn more. I pulled out my phone and began to dial.

"Kayla? What are you doing out here? It's freezing; come inside before you catch a cold. Aunt Sandra and the rest of the family are on their way for Boxing Day celebrations. It would help if you got ready," Mum cheered. She was still very much in the Christmas spirit.

It was her favourite time of year, and she loved planning events for the whole family to get together. If Aunt Sandra was on her way, my favourite cousin, Crystal, was on her way too. She was older than me; she would know what to do about Connor.

"Coming, Mum!" I smiled, stuffing the card back in my pocket with my phone and running inside.

"Sandra! Girls! So glad you could come," Mum cheered, hugging everyone eagerly at the door.

"And miss your famous Boxing Day party? Never!" Aunt Sandra smiled, squeezing Mum tightly and handing her a bottle of red wine – like she did every year.

It wasn't long before relatives from both sides of my family showed up, and the house was booming. Music filled every room, and laughter and cheers filled the air. My younger cousins played in Andy's room with all his new toys. Dad was 'merry' and had taken to singing karaoke into Mum's hairbrush in the middle of the living room.

At times like this, I realised how lucky I was to have such a big and close family. It was about two hours into the party when my cousin Crystal arrived. She pulled up in her new red sports car and strode into the house looking like a superstar. She was always so glamorous and one of my favourite people.

"Hey, sorry I'm late. I got stuck at a work meeting. But the party can officially get started now that I'm here," Crystal exclaimed as she air-kissed each of us.

"Work on Boxing Day?" Uncle Brian groaned, wrapping Crystal into a hug. She immediately checked that her outfit was still well-pressed while keeping a megawatt smile on her gorgeous face.

"Joys of being a lawyer, Uncle B. The work doesn't stop just because of the holidays."

Once she had greeted everyone and poured herself a glass of Mum's famous Boxing Day punch, I grabbed her hand and pulled her away from the crowd to a relatively quiet part of the house.

"Hey, cuz. I take it you have some hot gossip for me?" Crystal laughed, kicking off her red stilettos and cuddling up with me in the bay window of the back room.

"I need your advice," I blurted out, aware that I had forgone any of the niceties we might have exchanged.

"Oooh, is it about a boy? Shoot! Give it to me; how can I help?" she asked excitedly.

I told her all about Christmas Eve. How Connor had bought me a coffee.... then bolted; how we were trapped in the lift and shared a suspended moment in time. How we had connected, and he gave me all the feels. How we kissed, and he disappeared.

Crystal sat listening intently. I told her about how he had been scared of missing a work thing. Being a workaholic herself, she understood. I told her how his eyes had glowed in a way I couldn't explain.

"Then, on Christmas morning, Andy found this under the tree." I handed her the card and pulled up the picture of the reindeer cookie on my phone.

"Cute, it matches the suit he bought," she grinned.

"Crystal!" I insisted.

"I'm sorry," she laughed. "What does he do for work again?"

"He didn't say, but I assume it is holiday-related."

"Okay, so let's look at this objectively. It was Christmas Eve; he was in a rush for a work event he couldn't miss. His family works with reindeer, and his number turns up in a box under your tree on Christmas morning. Huh! Maybe he is one of Santa's elves!"

I looked at Crystal with annoyance; I didn't like her mocking me.

"Look, do you like the guy?" she asked, taking a sip of her punch.

I nodded, a little too vigorously than what was considered cool. But this was Crystal; she wouldn't judge.

"Then call him. What's the worst that can happen?" She winked as she left to welcome her boyfriend to the party.

I sat looking out the window, watching as he got out of his car. Crystal ran outside, wrapping her arms around him and guiding him inside. Christmas elf? I doubted it. But I couldn't shake the feeling that somehow, though I couldn't explain it, Christmas magic was involved. I picked up my phone and stared at the card, still questioning if I should call.

CONNOR

Christmas night had been an enormous success. We made record time, beating the best around-the-world trip record held by the Blitzen family for almost a hundred years. I did such a good job leading the sleigh that Santa granted me a wish. I told him the story of Kayla and how I had left her without passing her my number. With a 'Ho-Ho-Ho,' he waved his hand and presented me with a box decorated to match my suit with a reindeer cookie and blank card.

"Write her a message, and I shall deliver it," Santa beamed.

"Thank you, Santa," I grinned back.

"You earned it tonight, Connor. You have restored your family name. You should be proud."

To hear that from the man himself, to say I was proud was an understatement. I couldn't wait to get home and tell my parents.

As we approached the North Pole again, I marveled at the sight below. Most humans imagined a simple workshop, but the reality was so much more impressive. From above, I could see the golden lights of the village stretching out in all directions, with buildings of various sizes nestled between towering evergreens. In the distance stood the imposing silhouette of a grand structure that I recognized as the main hall of North Pole University, where many shifters and magical beings studied the arts of holiday magic and seasonal balance.

"Beautiful, isn't it?" one of the other reindeer shifters said beside me. "Maybe you'll be attending NPU next year. After tonight's performance, I'd say you've got a good chance."

I nodded, allowing myself to hope. The university represented everything I'd ever dreamed of—a chance to learn more about my heritage, to develop my abilities, and perhaps most importantly, to continue restoring my family's reputation.

Sunrise was a few hours away. The time between completing the present drop and sunrise was Santa, the reindeer, and the elves' time to party. Our families would join us for another celebration come sunrise.

Arriving at Santa's workshop, we packed up the sleigh and our harnesses and headed back for the feast. Changed back into my suit, I walked into the dining hall to a round of thunderous applause. Confetti cannons popped and trumpets hooted. All my fellow shifters lined up, clapping their congratulations and patting me on the back. It was a dream come true, yet I felt deflated. Something was missing, and I couldn't place what it was.

We feasted, and the elves formed their band and played us out until sunrise. I even had the honour of a dance with Mrs Claus.

"I'm so proud of you, son. Your grandfather would be proud too." Dad smiled with tears of joy in his eyes as he pulled me into a hug.

Dad wasn't a hugger, so this was a pretty big deal. Even Mum and my sister were shocked. I was even more shocked when my sister paid me a compliment.

"Not bad. Maybe I should enter the reindeer games next year. You know, follow in my little brother's hoof prints." She winked before running off with her friends.

"My boy.... I..." Mum stuttered, tears drifting down her face.

"I love you too, Mum." I laughed, hugging her tightly.

As Boxing Day went on, discussions turned to next year's preparations and what the reindeer games would look like next year. Things were always nonstop at the North Pole. But as the celebrations continued, I found that I couldn't stop checking my phone. I wondered if Kayla had received my message, if she had realised that it was from me, and if she was going to call.

I snuck off to the barns and relaxed in the hay bales thinking about Kayla. Her eyes, her smile, and the small row of freckles across her nose. She had been so kind to me when I had left her in the lurch. She was something special.

"Hey, what's up? When I saw you sneak off from a party in your honour, I knew something had to be wrong," Samantha said, joining me in the barn and offering me a glass of peppermint punch – a shifter's favourite.

"I'm fine. It's just been a long night. I'm tired," I lied.

"Connor? Come on," she urged as she shoulder-bumped me.

"What makes you so sure something is wrong?"

"Call it big sister intuition. Now spill," she insisted.

I never could hide anything from Samantha; she was the best big sister a shifter could ask for. I had already told my family about Kayla the night before, just before I headed through our family portal. I explained that I feared even a message blessed with a bit of Christmas magic wouldn't be enough, and I had ruined things with her before they even had a chance to get started.

"I mean, I can't blame her for not calling. I didn't just up and leave once, but twice. And right after we kissed," I said, cringing at the memory.

"Wait! You neglected to tell us that part of the story last night," Samantha said, almost choking on her drink.

"Yeah, we kissed. And it was like it broke the spell. The lift doors opened, and I bolted. I just left her there. Santa granted me a wish last night...."

"Santa granted you a wish? What did you wish for?" Samantha asked excitedly.

"I wished for Kayla to have my number. He left it on a card wrapped around the neck of a reindeer cookie. I thought it was a sweet touch," I said with a smile.

"You big, soppy hopeless romantic, you. Of all the things you could wish for, you wish for *that*? You do realise that Santa doesn't offer wishes out to just anyone. I can't remember the last time he offered a wish, for that matter," she replied, tapping her upper lip.

"Sam, come on, it was my wish. I led his sleigh, restored our family name, and won the reindeer games. What more could I wish for? I have everything.... but the girl!"

"Fair point. Hold tight, little brother. If she is as special as you say, she will see the magic in you that we see every day." Samantha patted me on the head and ruffled my hair, the same way she had since we were kids.

Samantha returned to the party, leaving me with my thoughts as I watched the sunset over the North Pole. Day turned to night as the last orange glow of the sun descended over the snow-topped hills and the moon shone brightly from above. I felt all my hopes of ever hearing from Kayla begin to fade.

I plastered a fake smile on my face and headed back to the

party. It wouldn't do for the star reindeer to be absent too long. I felt my phone buzz in my pocket. Pulling it out, I checked the number; it was a number I didn't recognise. The magic within me churned.

"Hello?" I answered tentatively.

"Connor? It's Kayla. I don't know how, but I found your number under my Christmas tree," she said. I couldn't help but smile.

"Let's call it a bit of Christmas magic. I'm so glad you called."

7

KAYLA

We talked for hours about how our Christmas Days went and arranged for a date the following day. He made me laugh when he promised not to bolt this time. The more we talked, all nerves and reservations about taking a chance on Connor vanished on the winter wind. I wished him a good night and ended the call.

As soon as I got off the phone, I ran through the house, still bustling with family members, on the hunt for Crystal. She was on the phone in the kitchen when I found her, most likely with a client. I hoped to be as happy and successful as her one day.

"Hey, cuz, you look happier than you did earlier," she said as she ended the call.

"I called him," I told her as I stopped in front of her, panting from my mad dash.

"And...?"

"We're going on a date tomorrow. I'm so nervous," I admitted.

"Unsurprising, considering how your first encounter went. But let me tell you this: First impressions are sometimes not all that important. Give the boy a chance. You never know. You may embark on a magical romance."

She placed her hands on my shoulders and guided me to my room to help pick the perfect outfit. Our date was set for Jessie's café. I thought it poetic to have our first official date where it all started. After combing through my wardrobe, Crystal shook her head.

"None of these will do."

"I like my clothes," I retorted.

"There is nothing wrong with your clothes, but we need something special for this date. I'll be right back," she said.

Crystal went out to her car and came back with a suitcase. She had recently been travelling for work. She grabbed a blue skater skirt, a grey and black t-shirt with lace trim and my favourite black ankle boots. She pulled out her black Gucci belt and a few jewellery pieces and stepped back to look at the outfit.

"Something's missing.... Wait! I know," she said, emptying the contents of her suitcase on my bed.

"Here," she exclaimed, brandishing her 'lucky' leather jacket.

I had always admired Crystal's fashion sense and knew how much she loved that jacket. It meant a lot that she trusted me with it for my big date.

I stood outside the department store, anxiously pulling my scarf tighter to shield myself against the cold. Connor was running five minutes late, and I worried he might have decided against the date altogether.

After another five minutes, I'd had it. I pulled out my phone to text Crystal it was a bust when he ran straight into me, catching me by the shoulders to steady me.

I was ready to snap at him until I looked into his emerald eyes. They seemed brighter than I remembered, and I was hit with the same magical feeling I had when I first laid eyes on him.

"Hi," I breathed.

"Hi," he said, then blinked and went on, "So sorry I'm late. Traffic was awful, and I left my phone....at the office." He gave me what had to be his most charming apologetic look. It totally worked.

"I was starting to think you weren't coming," I admitted.

He brushed my hair behind my ear and looked me dead in the eye, "I messed up once; I don't intend to do it again. Mint Chocolate Mocha, right? That's if they are still serving the Christmas menu," he said, offering me his arm.

The date was terrific; we shared the same taste in music, movies, and books. We both were very close with our families. I told him about my plans to go to college and study law like my cousin Crystal and that I hoped to move to L.A. one day.

Connor was much more relaxed than during our conversation in the lift, but I still felt like he was holding back. The way he paused before he said things made me feel like he was hiding something. Like he was constantly measuring his words, ensuring that he said just enough to keep me interested but not too much that he might give something away. It was a little off-putting.

He stammered when I called him on it and replied, "You're right. I'm not used to spending time with people outside my circle. It makes me awkward."

It was a genuine response, but what did it even mean?

Connor sat fiddling with his spoon. Was this a red flag? If I let it slide, would my picture be in tomorrow's newspaper under the headline "*Missing London girl found dead in an alley off Oxford Street*"?

Stop being dramatic, Kayla.

"It's fine. We have all the time in the world to get to know each other," I replied, and I was happy to see his shoulders relax as he sighed in relief.

"So, is it safe to say a second date might be in the cards?" he asked, his gaze hopeful.

"If you play your cards right," I answered, amazed at my own cheek.

"I'm an excellent card player," he replied, eyes twinkling in merriment.

My heart skipped a beat when his smile met mine.

Once we had finished our drinks, we decided that it was time to go. It was getting late, and my house was still full of guests that I'd be disturbing if I came in during the wee hours.

While waiting for my Uber to arrive, we agreed to catch a movie the following night. The new James Bond movie was out, and we were both excited to see it.

When my car arrived, I wished him good night. He opened the car door, but before I could slip in, he took my arm and leaned in close. Really close.

As though his proximity hadn't tipped me off, he whispered, "Is it okay if I kiss you goodnight?"

I smiled, my heart nearly knocking the breath out of me, but I managed to reply, "You don't have to ask every time."

To prove my point, I grabbed onto the lapels of his jacket and pulled him closer, pressing my lips to his. He tasted like ginger-bread and peppermint, and for a minute, it felt like we were spinning. This kiss was as magical as our first, except that when I opened my eyes, he was still there. I smiled. He smiled. The Uber driver barked, "Are ye getting in!?"

We burst out laughing. Connor kissed my forehead and ushered me into the car. "See you tomorrow," he said as he closed the door.

I waved at him as the car pulled away, unable to stop the goofy grin that spread from ear to ear. When I couldn't see him anymore, I checked my phone, hoping that he might have texted me. He hadn't, but Crystal had.

Crystal: So, how did it go?

I had no patience for texting, so I called her instead. She answered on the first ring.

"So? Did my lucky jacket work?" she asked, and I could hear her smile through the phone.

"It did," I answered with a giggle.

"I take it things went well?"

"It was.... magical," I said, resting my head on the frozen window. I couldn't feel the chill at all.

CONNOR

Waiting outside the movie theatre, I couldn't believe my luck. I had achieved my goal and got a second date with this beautiful girl. Dreams really did come true! The more I got to know Kayla, the more challenging it became to keep my secret. I wondered how long it would be before I either slipped up, scared her off, or lost her trust entirely.

"Hi, I hope you haven't been waiting long," I heard her say as she walked out of a sleek red sports car. Immediately, my hackles raised until I saw a gorgeous woman waving at me from the driver's seat. I put a hand up as I shifted my gaze to Kayla.

Both the car and woman were forgotten in an instant as I took in the oceanic depths of Kayla's eyes. All my worries about revealing my secret dispersed. It would keep a while longer.

I debated kissing her again, but was a little intimidated by Kayla's ride. So, I placed a hand on the small of her back and ushered her into the movie theatre. I bought the tickets and let Kayla choose the snacks. When she insisted on paying for them, I smiled and thanked her. Samantha had warned me that there might be a test such as this.

We found our seats, and she tucked into me naturally. I didn't even have to sneak an arm around her. It felt right having her there.

I wish I could say that the movie was great, but I was too distracted by Kayla. She was totally engrossed in the film, grabbing my arm during the action scenes, sighing at the romantic bits, and laughing out loud at the one-liners. She was the show I'd pay to see every day. She enjoyed it, and that's all that mattered.

"I'm so glad we did this," she said as we left the cinema.

"Me too. So, I guess you enjoyed the movie?" I asked, tongue-in-cheek, but she missed the sarcasm entirely. She went on about her favourite parts of the movie, and all I could do was smile and nod, delighted by her effervescence.

"What shall we do for our third date?" I asked, hoping she would go for it.

"My best friend Louise is having a party on New Year's Eve if you want to come," she replied excitedly.

New Year's Eve and New Year's Day were always big at the North Pole. It was when Santa handed out the high achiever awards, and everyone got their annual duties. There was always a feast, and the elves put on a talent show – they were complete show-offs, but, in their defence, we were the only audience they could play for. I wanted to go with her and meet her friends, but I already had plans.

"I would love to meet your friends," I said honestly.

"So, you will come?" she asked, and her eyes lit up like the first morning of spring.

"I wish I could, but I have plans with family. Maybe we could go to dinner after the New Year, and you could bring Louise," I suggested.

Her face fell, and she said, "Sure, we can do that."

She checked her watch and said she should text her cousin before it got too late.

"I'll wait with you until she gets here," I replied.

She must have been on her way already because we barely had time to throw around some restaurant ideas before the red sports car was back. I opened the car door for her but felt too self-conscious to kiss her with an audience. Either she felt the same way, or I had blown it big time because she gave me a peck on the cheek and told me to call her in a few days.

8

KAYLA

I felt bad for how things ended. Sure, I was disappointed that Connor had plans on New Year's Eve, but honestly, could I really be surprised that he had plans? Who didn't?

Once I'd gone over the date with Crystal and said goodnight, I lay in bed wondering what to do. If I didn't reach out to him now, he might think I wasn't interested anymore.

I sat up in bed, grabbed my phone, and shot him a quick text.

> Me: I had a lovely time tonight. I know you have plans tomorrow night, but perhaps we could go for a walk at some point during the day?

I waited for what seemed like an eternity. When it didn't look like he would respond, I put my phone back on the nightstand. *He's probably already asleep*. I tried to get comfortable, but kept tossing and turning, thinking I had ruined everything.

When I heard the tell-tale ping, I pounced on my phone.

> Connor: I'm so happy you texted. Had a great time too. How about Richmond Park at eleven?

I pumped my legs in the air and squealed into a pillow.

> Me: I'll meet you there. Goodnight, Connor.

> Connor: Goodnight, Kayla.

How I ever managed to fall asleep is anybody's guess. When I woke up the next day, the sun shone, and life was good.

I had breakfast with my family and took a train to Richmond Park. When I arrived, Connor was waiting for me at the pedestrian gate at Petersham. I ran up to him and stopped abruptly in front of him when I realised that I was being much too eager. As Connor was grinning like a loon, I figured that he, too, was happy to see me.

We stood awkwardly, unsure of how to greet one another. Then, Connor took the lead and wrapped me in a hug.

"Good morning, Kayla," he said, his warm breath near my ear.

"Good morning, Connor," I replied, a little breathless.

When we pulled apart, I asked him what was in the backpack.

"It takes about three hours to walk the entire park. I figured we'd get hungry. And I also brought extra clothes in case we got cold," he said.

"Wow, you came prepared. Is this where you take all the girls on a winter hike?" I asked, giving him a shoulder bump.

He turned pink, and the look of utter dismay he wore told me everything I needed to know.

"I swear, I've never taken a girl here. Other than my sister, but I don't think that's what you meant."

"It's okay. I was only kidding. You should see the look on your face!" I teased.

He motioned toward the path, and I fell into step with him.

"I come here a lot with my parents," he said.

"That's right. You have a deer farm," I said.

"It's more of a deer conservation preserve than a farm, but yes. They cull the deer in Richmond Park twice a year, the females in November and the males in February. The park is closed to the public then."

I stopped walking and looked at him.

"Cull...as in kill? They hunt the deer in Richmond Park?"

He sighed and ran a hand over his face. "Yes and no. Culling is necessary to keep the herd healthy and avoid overpopulation, which may lead to deer dying of starvation. The deer that are culled are sold to game wholesalers. The money is then used to maintain the deer and the park. We try to buy a few every year so they can live out their days in peace. I wish we could take them all, but they are worth more as meat, so it gets expensive."

"I had no idea. That's so sad. I know why it's important, but I can't stand the idea of animals being killed. Can't they all be relocated, or released in the wild somewhere else?" I asked.

"No, they wouldn't survive." Connor took my hand and kissed my cheek. "Cheer up. I know it's sad, but there are others like us who buy the culled deer. We save as many as we can. Come on, let's go see them."

We continued the path, and Connor asked me about school. I was happy with the change of topic.

A little after noon, Connor asked if I was hungry. I said that I was, and we found a bench to have our picnic.

Connor had thought of everything. He draped a heavy blanket

over the bench so we wouldn't get cold. He had a thermos of hot tomato soup, sharp cheese cut into cubes, and tiny baguettes. Next, he pulled out another thermos, this one filled with minty hot chocolate. He offered me a tin filled with the most beautifully decorated Christmas cookies I had ever seen. They were even prettier than the ones Claude made at the bakery.

"Thanks for the picnic, Connor. Everything was delicious," I said as we packed everything back into his backpack.

When we resumed our walk, I shivered from the cold.

"Hey, are you okay?" asked Connor.

"I feel chillier than before," I said, zipping up my coat and pulling my hat down over my ears.

"That's because we stopped moving for a while. Come here, let me warm you up," he replied as he opened his arms for a hug. I stepped into his embrace and, despite our heavy coats, I started getting warmer.

Connor pressed in a little while kissing my hair, then my cheek. He slowly left a trail of them until he reached my lips. The world was spinning again, and it was amazing. We stood kissing and kissing. I wasn't cold anymore. In fact, as our tongues met and danced, it got downright steamy.

When the snow started falling, we kept on kissing. A snowflake fluttered onto my eyelashes, and I opened my eyes to dislodge it. That's when I caught a movement behind Connor. I thought it might be other patrons, so I pulled back to let Connor know we were making a spectacle of ourselves.

But it wasn't other people coming our way. It was a deer. And he wasn't ambling in our direction; he looked like he was charging at us.

I started hitting Connor's chest and yelling, "Deer, deer, deer!"

Connor kissed the top of my nose and replied, "They're beautiful, right?"

I pushed his shoulders so he would turn around. "No, it's coming right at us!" I screeched.

Connor pushed me behind him and told me not to move or say anything. I was terrified. I knew he was used to dealing with deer, but I was pretty sure you shouldn't face off against a charging deer. I put a hand on my mouth to keep from screaming as I watched Connor take a few steps forward and growl at the deer. The deer wasn't fazed and kept coming.

Suddenly, a golden mist surrounded Connor, and I heard a grunt. What stood before me was something I never expected to see.

CONNOR

The buck wouldn't back down. I shifted and rushed him, growling to assert dominance. When he didn't so much as pause, I charged. I'd never charged a regular deer before, and I hoped they reacted the same way shifters did. It was basically a game of chicken. The first to veer away lost. If both continued, there would be a battle with antlers, and I wasn't sure I'd be the victor if it came to that.

Fortunately, it didn't. My charge was enough to spook the buck, and he ran back to the herd. I turned to Kayla. She was safe. Moreover, she hadn't bolted at the sight of me. My nostrils flared as I checked the park for prying eyes. It wouldn't do to be caught out in the open in my reindeer form. Worse yet, to be caught on camera.

Kayla moved slowly towards me, her hand out like I was a strange dog. "Shhh, Connor, it's okay, it's just me. No one else is here," she soothed. She calmed me the way that she had in the lift.

She reached out to stroke my head. I took a step back, worried. Looking into her eyes that matched the sky, I knew deep down that I could trust her. I nudged her hand with my nose and allowed her to stroke my head.

I could tell she had questions. She opened her mouth to speak a few times, but no sound came out. Stepping away, I shifted back, self-conscious about having her watch me.

"I guess you have a few questions."

"A few, yeah," she breathed.

I stood in front of her patiently, hoping and praying that she wouldn't run scared, or worse, reveal my secret to the rest of the world. In a way, I was relieved the cat was out of the bag – or rather, the reindeer was out of the sack. I suppose seeing is believing, and it was better for her to see it with her own eyes than for me to try and explain it to her.

"I don't know what set him off. He was probably jealous that I was kissing such a pretty girl," I said, trying to lighten the mood.

She laughed and suggested that we double back. She threaded her gloved fingers through mine, and we walked back to the tube station.

"Don't worry, your secret is safe with me. It's just a lot to get my head around, and I need some time to think," she said.

"I get it; it's a lot. And I trust you," I said. I gave her a big hug and she kissed my cheek before she left. I really hoped I hadn't blown my chance with her.

9
KAYLA

I took the world's longest shower when I got home. I was frozen to the bone, and I had some thinking to do. I replayed every single moment since I had met Connor, and things started to make sense. The way his eyes glowed on Christmas Eve, his fear of being trapped in the lift, how he found the reindeer cookie funny, and how his number ended up under my tree. But I still needed to know more.

I knew that he would be busy tonight and tomorrow. If I waited, I wouldn't get any answers. There was a lot going on here too. But I just couldn't put it out of my mind.

Still wrapped in my towel, I texted Connor.

Me: Can we meet? We need to talk.

He replied instantly.

Connor: Of course. Just tell me where and when. I'll be there.

We met at Jessie's café. Connor was there when I arrived, his right leg bouncing nervously under the table as he shredded a napkin absently. When he saw me, his face lit up, and he stood.

"Kayla, you came," he said, wrapping me in a hug.

"Of course, I came. It was my idea." I laughed, swatting him on the arm. "Should we sit? Is it better to go outside?" I whispered.

"No, this is fine. There's enough background music and chatter that we won't be overheard," he replied. "Do you want anything to eat or drink?"

"No, I'm still full from our picnic."

Had that only been a few hours ago?

Connor took a deep breath and explained everything. My skin prickled hearing it all; some of it would be hard to believe. But after what I saw in the park, there was no way any of it was a lie. He told me about the reindeer games, his family history, and the 'work' event that had him running on Christmas Eve.

"I should be scared. This is incredible. But I'm.... fascinated. This is so...."

"Magical?" Connor asked with a mischievous look on his face.

"Yes." I laughed. "Have you ever told anyone else?"

"Not a soul. And I'm not supposed to either."

"Why?" I asked.

"The rest of the world is not as understanding as you. It's better for the world that only the innocent truly experience the magic of Christmas."

"I may be under 18, but I'm not a kid," I protested.

"No, but you're an innocent. Innocents can be anywhere from 2 to 102," he replied.

I had many questions, and Connor was more than happy to answer them. It turned out that very few people worldwide knew of the magic that surrounded them on a daily basis. The more he told me, the more I felt my belief in magic and Christmas returning. It was like I could feel the magic running through my veins; I could feel its energy.

"So magic is everywhere?" I asked.

"Come on, let me show you," Connor smiled, offering me his hand.

We went out to the street, and Connor pointed out the magic happening under our very noses. I never realized just how much magic I witnessed daily but never truly saw.

Now that I'd reawakened my childhood innocence, I saw it everywhere! I recognized shifters by the glow in their eyes; people using magic had strings of glowing thread surrounding their every move. Twinkle lights not only twinkled but also emitted a faint chime as they swayed in the wind.

"I feel so foolish," I sighed.

"Why?"

"I've taken so much for granted, never appreciated the world around me. The magic is real!"

"Belief in magic fades as we grow older; it's not foolish. But now you know, and you can see."

I felt more connected to Connor than ever. He had shared his deepest secret with me, trusted me with such important information, and gave me so much more than he could ever know.

My mind was already cataloging everything I was seeing, wondering about the history behind it all. "Has anyone ever documented how these magical traditions began? Are there books about magical law and history?" I asked, my academic curiosity piqued. "I mean, there must be records somewhere, right?"

Connor looked surprised but pleased by my questions. "There's a whole library at North Pole University dedicated to magical history. Some of the texts go back thousands of years."

"A magical university?" I breathed, excitement building. "That sounds fascinating. I'd love to read those books someday."

I felt more connected to Connor than ever. He had shared his deepest secret with me, trusted me with such important information, and gave me so much more than he could ever know. Belief. It is a simple thing that we take for granted, but something that can truly enrich and change our lives.

"So, New Year's Eve. What will you be up to?" I asked.

"A big awards ceremony and New Year's celebration at the North Pole," Connor answered.

"Do you think you'll get an award?" I asked, hoping I was being subtle enough. I wanted to go; I wanted to see it all for myself. To experience the authentic, breathing magic of Christmas.

"I am nominated for a few, yes," Connor replied, beaming with pride.

"So, it's an intimate gathering, just for reindeer shifters?" I asked.

"No, the elves and Santa will be there, of course," he replied.

"Of course!"

Connor stopped walking and pulled me out of the way of passers-by.

"Kayla, can I ask you something?"

"Yes, you can kiss me," I said as I puckered up, checking to see if he'd pulled me under the mistletoe.

Connor smiled and kissed me gently. This kiss was extraordinary; I could literally feel sparks when our lips met, and my heart started to beat really fast. I was falling for this boy, this... reindeer shifter.

He pulled back, brushing a stray hair behind my ear.

"Kayla, would you be my date for the New Year's Eve awards ceremony?"

"I thought you'd never ask!"

10

KAYLA

There wasn't much time to prepare. Louise was going to kill me. I chewed the inside of my cheek while I thought about how to tell my best friend I was ditching her for a guy. A guy I had barely told her about. It all happened so fast, and with my cousin Crystal at home, Louise and I hadn't been in as close contact as we usually were.

It would be nice to go over to her house and explain everything. But it was past four, and Connor would pick me up at eight. I still had to have dinner with the fam, put on my glam, and, if I could find the time, chill out.

Not only was I going on another date with the cutest boy ever, but it was a New Year's Eve gala hosted by Santa at the North Pole. If that weren't nerve-wracking enough, I'd also be meeting Connor's parents, sister, and all his reindeer friends.

To think I'd been complaining about how dull my holiday break was going to be. Trust me to find the most complicated boy to date.

No, I would have to text Louise and prepare to grovel for

forgiveness when I saw her again. I took a minute to word it as best as possible and pressed send. Thankfully, she did not respond immediately, and I could focus on the ensuing problem. Mum and Dad.

There was no way they would let me travel to the North Pole with strangers and spend the night. I laughed out loud at the absurdity and got sour looks from my fellow tube riders. I mouthed an apology and saw it was time to get off.

As I walked home from the station, I texted Crystal. It kept my eyes out of the path of the freezing wind, though my fingers weren't spared.

Me: S.O.S

Crystal: What's up?

Me: Connor invited me to a fancy NYE party. I will need to stay over. Thoughts?

Crystal: Weren't you going to a party and sleeping over, anyway?

Me: Yes, at Louise's. But…

Crystal: Where are you?

Me: Two doors down.

Crystal: Be home in 15.

When I got home, Mum and Aunt Sandra were in the kitchen peeling turnips and carrots for dinner. I gave them each a quick peck on the cheek and made for my room. On the way, I stopped in on Andy; he and the younger cousins were playing Super Mario Bros on the console. I said hi and got a collective "yo!" back.

In my room, it was time to address yet another issue. Louise and I had bought killer dresses for tonight's shindig. Mine was a black sequin blouson sleeve shift dress. A tad short for me, but Louise had insisted the dress had simple lines and was flattering. I'd gone for it because it was comfortable and looked good with trainers. There was a matching clutch and voila. Outfit sorted.

The problem was that when I asked Connor about the dress code, he said, "Anything but black. Red, white, and green are the 'in' colours."

"Will you be wearing your green tartan suit?" I asked in reply.

"No, that was a special outfit for Santa's dinner party. I'll wear a tailored forest green velvet dress jacket, a crisp white shirt, a bowtie, and matching green herringbone trousers."

I stared at him open-mouthed.

"You're really into clothes, aren't you?" I asked nervously. Clearly, the trainers were out. I'd have to wear proper heels.

He chuckled and waved that away. "I hate shopping. The tartan suit was the first clothes I'd ever bought for myself. My sister Sam does all my shopping."

"You described your outfit with more detail than my friend Louise would ever use," I said, colour returning to my face.

"I was told to memorize it before I came to meet you in case you asked me what I was wearing," he explained, and I sagged with relief.

A knock at the door brought me back to the here and now.

"Hey, Luv. Have you sorted what you'll wear tonight?" asked Crystal as she breezed into my room. It was already after five, and I could smell the tantalizing aroma of Beef Wellington wafting in with her. Dinner was at six, and I needed to be party-ready as there wouldn't be enough time after the meal.

I grabbed the dress and the clutch from the closet and showed them to Crystal. "I was meant to wear this tonight, but apparently, black is not an option."

Crystal took the hanger and placed the dress in front of her as she gazed in the mirror. "We can switch. You can wear mine. It's red!" she said with a wink. My stomach sank. It was either fanny short, cut to the navel, or slit to the unmentionables.

She rolled her eyes at me. "Not my party dress, my dinner dress." She hung the dress in my wardrobe and pulled me into her room. Once there, she produced two red dresses. One was a flaming red backless satin shift dress, aka the party dress. The thing was barely more than a napkin held by a ribbon. I shuddered.

The other was a cerise red with a halter neck, lace top bodice, and a high-waisted chiffon skirt. I was prim and proper. I narrowed my eyes at her; when would Crystal ever wear a dress like this?

"Try it on," she urged, producing a matching lace evening clutch.

I stripped out of my t-shirt and jeans and slipped into the dress. Crystal zipped up my back and put my hair up with a clip. The dress fit perfectly, too perfectly. Our eyes met in the mirror; mine were welling up. She bought this dress for me.

"How?" I choked. "How did you know?"

She wrapped me in a hug and scoffed. "I was shopping the sales in town and came across this little beauty. I was sure you had a dress for tonight, but something told me to get it. They were practically giving it away," she said as she reached for a box under the bed.

Crystal opened the lid and presented it to me. Gingerly, I lifted the tissue paper to reveal a pair of red suede Mary Jane shoes with block heels the same shade as the dress. I stood there stroking the soft suede in reverence.

"Go on, try 'em on!"

I shook myself out of the trance and grabbed the shoes out of the box. I rolled off my fuzzy socks and slipped into the shoes—perfect fit and so comfortable.

"Let's have a look," said Crystal as she handed me the clutch. She looked me over critically, then gave a satisfied nod. "A bit of gloss and those tear-drop earrings you wore at Christmas, and you're all set."

She was right. I looked amazing. I beamed at myself in the mirror, and then I remembered I still had to get past Mum and Dad.

"Why the long face, Luv?" asked Crystal.

"What do I say to Mum and Dad?"

Crystal tapped a finger on her upper lip. "How are you getting there?" she asked, then scrunching her face, she added, "Where are you going exactly?"

Connor and I hadn't discussed what I could and couldn't reveal. All I knew was that even I wasn't supposed to know that he was a shifter. I was pretty sure telling Crystal about the North Pole wasn't allowed.

"He's coming to pick me up and take me back to his house. He lives in Richmond," I said. That was true.

"Does he have a car?" she asked.

"I don't think so," I replied.

"I'm assuming he's being chivalrous, but it makes no sense for him to come all the way here only to head back."

I merely shrugged.

"Go have a shower, and I'll think about it," she said, waving me out of her room.

CONNOR

"You can take the time to chew your food, Luv," Mum said at dinner. "Especially since Kayla's cousin is driving her over. There's plenty of time."

"I can't wait to meet her," said Samantha.

"She must be quite the young lady for Santa to agree to her being your escort to the ball," said Dad. "You did clear this with the big guy, right?"

He was justifiably worried. The Prancers had just cleared their name at the North Pole, and no one wanted to make any waves.

"Yes, Dad. Santa knows all about Kayla. Besides, plenty of shifters will have dates," I replied.

"Dates they're in serious relationships with. Dates who have taken the oath," replied Dad solemnly.

"I know I haven't known Kayla for very long, and I can't even say we're in any relationship, but I know I can trust her. Besides, she's an innocent. Doesn't that count for something?" I asked. My voice cracked on the last bit, and I cleared my throat.

Mum placed a hand over mine and squeezed. "She must be exceptional, indeed."

I'd never brought anyone home and told no one I was a shifter. Not even Paul, my closest friend at school. I'd turned less than a year ago and never felt the need or the urge to tell anyone. I'd made friends at the Pole. We had more in common, even if our everyday lives were different.

Now that I had joined Santa's line-up, I was part of a pack. Unless I messed up, I would stay in the pack until I had a family or I turned 25, whichever came first.

As though reading my thoughts, Sam asked if I was planning to transfer after the holidays.

"I think so," I said. "Besides Paul, I don't have that many friends at school that I would miss, and Paul lives down the lane. We'll stay in touch."

"Won't switching schools mid-year strain your studies?" asked Mum.

"I'm no genius, but I do all right. I can't imagine school at the Pole will be harder than at St. Paul's."

"I should think not, but we know little about the quality of the education you'll receive there," said Mum. "Your dad's never been, nor has anyone in our family still alive to tell us about it."

"True, but I've heard great things. Besides, it's free. Think of the money you'll save!"

"Don't worry, Petra. I've heard great things, too. The important thing is that he is well-trained for his reindeer duties. Santa's pack members usually go on to Oxford or Cambridge. They wouldn't get in if the school were inadequate," Dad said.

He sat back in his chair, hands braced on the table. He wore a satisfied smile and sighed. But I also saw a gleam in his eye and wondered if he might not be a little envious. He turned to look at me, and I smiled, trying to convey that I understood I'd be attending for both of us. His responding wink told me he was grateful.

"All right then," said Mum. "If everyone's done, we'd best clear the table and get ready for our guests."

11

KAYLA

As we turned onto Fife Road, I understood why things had gone so smoothly at dinner when Crystal brought up the change of plans. When I said Connor lived in Richmond, my parents' smiles went up a notch, and they'd been entirely on board with Crystal's plan.

She would drive me to Connor's house, meet the boy and his parents and determine whether it was safe for me to be left in their care. If not, she'd take me back to Louise, where I'd stay as initially planned. If all went well, she would pick me up after brunch the next day on her way back from her own party.

"This is posher than I expected," Crystal said as we passed one gated mansion after another. When we reached Connor's address, I was relieved to find it was neither gated nor an estate. Granted, it was grossly six times the size of our townhouse, but it was modest compared to the other houses on the lane.

"Now I know why he goes to Richmond Park so often; it's literally in his backyard," I said.

Crystal and I checked our reflections before exiting the car. I turned to her before ringing the bell. "How do I look?"

"Fab. Absolutely fab!" she replied, giving me a side squeeze.

Moments later, Connor opened the door. If I thought he looked handsome before, I had no words to describe the Burberry model that stood before me now. He smiled. I smiled.

"Hello! I'm cousin Crystal. You must be Connor!" my cousin said while holding out a perfectly manicured hand. She was giving him her megawatt smile; it was hard to resist.

"Hello, Crystal, Kayla, please come in," he said, moving to the side to let us pass.

He took our coats and hung them in a wardrobe nearby. He placed my backpack near the staircase. Faced with such luxury, it looked ridiculous. When he returned, he eyed Crystal as he inched closer to me. We stood awkwardly for a minute, still unsure how to greet one another, especially with an audience.

When we heard someone call out, "Is it Kayla and her cousin, Luv?" from another room, he quickly kissed my cheek and whispered, "You look lovely."

"So do you," I replied with a giggle.

"Come in, come in," said Connor's mum as she ushered us into the sitting room.

A fire was crackling in the massive fireplace, and the décor was everything I expected a grand house in a posh neighbourhood to be. Tasteful, sophisticated, yet comfortable and lived in.

"You have a beautiful home," said Crystal as she accepted a glass of sherry from Mister Prancer.

"Thank you," he replied. "It's been in our family for generations." He pointed to a portrait on the opposite wall. "That's my ancestor Burgess Prancer. We have passed the house down from father to son. One day, it'll be Connor's."

Crystal frowned. Ever the feminist, I could see she was about to object. I jumped in and asked, "So, is the party here in Richmond?

Connor and I hadn't had time to discuss managing this part. All he'd said was that his father would take care of it.

"The ball is being held nearby, close enough to walk. If you'd like, Petra can show you the guest room to ensure it's up to your standards," he replied a little too smoothly. But Crystal only beamed at him and replied, "That would be lovely!"

CONNOR

After Crystal left, satisfied that we would take proper care of her young cousin, I gave Kayla a more encompassing tour of the house, ending with my room.

"You're really into tartan, aren't you?" she asked, trailing her fingers over the wool throw at the end of my bed.

"I am. But *that* specific tartan is a family heirloom."

"Do you have Scottish roots, then?" she asked as she turned to face me, interested.

"Most people assume tartans are Scottish, but quite a few are British. This one is associated with Devon, where my ancestors were from."

She moved to my bookcase and inspected my books. She was about to pull out one of the books, but Mum called us down. It was time to go.

I took her hand and pulled her close. We may not have a moment alone for a few hours, and I'd been dying to kiss her.

Face to face, our hands still loosely clasped, I stared at this beautiful girl. I felt giddy at the sight of the goody grin she aimed at me; it matched my own. I loved that she wasn't wearing any lipstick. I moved in, and her lips parted in anticipation. There was a tingle when our mouths met. Not the kind you get from static. No, this felt like magic.

We kissed, and I swear I felt lifted off the ground while fairy dust spiralled around us. A thousand and one fireflies exploded in my gut. They swirled and rose, shooting up like champagne after you've shaken a bottle of Prosecco. When they reached my throat, I could barely breathe. Unable to contain them, I broke the kiss and let them out.

"I love you."

Horrified, I clasped a hand over my mouth. I hadn't meant to say that.

Eyes wide in surprise, Kayla was searching my face. Her lips were still parted, and I could see a faint smile. Whether from the kiss or the admission, it was hard to tell. The main thing was she hadn't flinched, or worse, fled.

"Quit snogging and come down, will you! Dad's about to have a coronary," came a voice from the door.

Kayla yelped, and Sam burst out laughing.

"In your own little world, weren't you?" She chuckled.

Kayla looked at her, dazed, then back at me.

"If you don't come with me, Kayla, you may never make it to the North Pole." My sister snorted as she pulled Kayla out of my room toward the stairs.

Mum and Dad were waiting in the sitting room. When we arrived, they stood.

"Does anyone need to visit the loo before we go?" Mum asked.

No one needed to go.

Dad took a small glass from the mantel and offered it to Kayla. She frowned and replied, "Oh, no, thank you. I'm underage, and I don't much care for spirits."

"I'm glad to hear it, dear, but this isn't alcohol. It's an oath," said Dad.

Kayla blinked and stared at Dad blankly. She looked to me for answers.

"As I told you, we're not supposed to tell outsiders we're shifters or that the North Pole truly exists. Before you can see it for yourself, you must take an oath," I explained, nodding at the glass of green liquid she had yet to accept.

"I'm confused. Isn't an oath like swearing on the bible or something?"

"That's how it used to be. But people don't have the same respect for the good book that they used to, so the Elves came up with something a tad more binding," said Mum.

"Drinking the Oath keeps you from revealing anything to anyone," added Sam.

"How?" asked Kayla.

"Tomorrow, when your cousin comes to pick you up, she'll likely ask about your evening. Should you decide to tell her you met Santa and danced with an elf, your cousin would hear something entirely different," replied Dad.

"Like what?" Kayla asked, bemused.

"Like you met a guy named Gary and danced with an ambassador or whatever would sound plausible to her ears," I said.

"But how will I know what to say?" asked Kayla, her brows bunching together.

"That's the beauty of it. You don't have to lie or make up a story. The magic in the potion will mask and morph your words," said Dad.

"That's brilliant!" she exclaimed.

"I'm glad you think so. Now, if you don't mind, we must be on our way," said Dad, pushing the glass into her hand. "Bottom's up!"

Kayla took the glass and sniffed.

"Best drink it in one go," said Sam.

Kayla nodded and drank it down like a shot. She made a face and handed the glass back to Dad. "It tastes better than cough syrup, but I wouldn't want another."

We all laughed, and Dad pulled the lever.

12

KAYLA

I hadn't recovered from the potion when Connor's dad pushed one stone from the fireplace. It popped out, and he pulled on it. Immediately, the floor shifted under my feet, and I stepped back.

I stared at it, trying to work out why part of the floor was spinning away from me. When I looked up, I understood. It was like in that Indiana Jones movie where the fireplace rotates.

When it stopped moving, I realized this fireplace, thankfully unlit, was much taller than the other.

"That is crackers!" I exclaimed.

Sam chuckled and followed her parents into the opening. Connor took my hand, and we went to stand next to them.

When Connor's dad pulled on a cord, I looked up. Would we shoot up the chimney?

I was disappointed to find no outlet above, but the fireplace spun again. This time, it opened into a large ballroom where the party was already in full swing. Men, women, and children were talking and dancing.

Like us, others were stepping out of fireplaces all about the room. Connor pulled the cord again, and the lit fireplace was back. "Never leave a fire unattended," he said with a wink.

"All right, children, you know the drill. The lights will blink fifteen minutes before the awards ceremony begins. Let's meet back here," said Connor's dad.

Everyone agreed, and Connor's parents went to join their friends. Sam did the same.

Connor turned to me and said, "I forgot to tell you before we left, but cell phones don't work here, nor do most watches. If you want to leave them here on the mantel, no one will take them, I promise."

I had been checking my smartwatch to determine what time it was here. That's when I remembered reading that the North Pole is the convergence of all time zones and was, therefore, out of time.

"But how will I contact Crystal or my parents if there's a problem?" I asked.

"There are analog phones in the lounge. You'll be patched through," he replied.

"How do they know what time the ceremony begins?"

"To make it easier on us, they use GMT, the same time as in London."

I nodded. As pretty as my clutch was, I would likely put it on a table somewhere and forget it. I slipped off my watch and dropped it inside. If I needed to refresh my gloss, I could just as quickly do it here than in the ladies' room. I took note of this particular fireplace and placed my bag on the mantel. With over fifty of them scattered around the room, it would be easy to get lost.

Connor offered his arm, and we headed toward a group of young people chatting near the stage.

As we neared, one of the older boys caught my eye and walked over.

He bowed and extended his hand, not to shake mine but to kiss it. I blushed and pulled it back quickly.

"What's a ravishing beauty like you doing with a runt like Connor?" he asked.

Though it was a compliment, I narrowed my eyes at him. "That's not a gracious thing to say about one of your mates."

The boy's hand flew to his chest, and he affected a wounded expression. "Ravishing and sharp!" he said. "Apologies. You misunderstand. Connor here is the newest and youngest member of the pack; he's the runt. It's a fact, not a slur."

Connor chuckled and introduced the arse. "This is Oliver Donner. He's the eldest, the pack leader. Calling me the runt is one of his privileges, though I think he enjoys it entirely too much."

I merely nodded. I made a mental note to ask if the pack leader was also the alpha, but I didn't want to embarrass Connor with stupid questions.

We moved closer to the others, and I was introduced to the ten other reindeer shifters and their dates. Two of the shifters were holding hands. I made another mental note to ask about the rules of the pack. Dating pack members seemed to be allowed.

"Nice to meet you, Kayla," said Spencer, Seraphina Blitzen's boyfriend. "If you have questions, I'm your guy. We normies need to stick together."

"Thanks," I said. I glanced at Seraphina, and she nodded in agreement.

We chatted, and some fizzy drinks were served. I don't think they had any alcohol, and they were tasty. Once I'd answered the group's questions - how old are you, where do you live, where do you go to school, how did you and Connor meet - the group seemed to lose interest and resumed their conversations.

"How long until the ceremony?" I asked. "Is there time for a tour?"

Connor turned toward the stage and pointed. "See that big hourglass?" he said, and I nodded. "It's how long we have until Santa arrives."

"Oh, then we should stick around," I replied, seeing very little sand left.

Connor chuckled. "That's the thing. It's a magical hourglass; the sand will speed up or slow down based on Santa's timeline. So, we never really know how long we have."

"That makes no sense!" I said, and Connor shrugged.

"To answer your question, we have time for a mini tour. When the lights blink, we'll head back. They won't start without us," he said.

CONNOR

I took Kayla out of the ballroom and into the hall, where a miniature of Santa's Village was showcased. I pointed to the tallest building on the southern side of town.

"We're on the ground floor of the school building. This is where all major events happen."

"School?" she asked.

"Shifter School," I replied. When she stared back at me blankly, I continued. "Once we join Santa's team, we're expected to attend school here."

"Like boarding school?"

"Yes, exactly like boarding school. We can go home at the weekend and Holidays."

She nodded and peered at the model. "What are these other buildings? Where's the workshop?"

Of course, she would ask about the workshop.

"Santa doesn't actually have a workshop, per se," I replied. This would be tricky to explain.

"Where do the elves make the toys and presents?" she asked.

Her face was so earnest, and I just had to kiss her then. She smiled and leaned into the kiss. No more than a heartbeat had passed before she put her hands on my chest and pushed away from me.

"Where are the elves? I didn't see them in the ballroom," she asked, eyes searching my face like she was afraid I would pull a fast one on her.

I sighed.

"The elves aren't cute little munchkins like you see in movies. They're shifters, and they don't make toys."

Her face fell. This is what I was dreading. She had such high hopes for the North Pole; the truth was bound to disappoint her.

"What?" she exclaimed, turning to the model. "What are all these buildings for, then? And what do the elves shift into or from?" She was panicking. I could tell she was mentally flipping through every book and movie she'd ever seen, trying to find an alternative to the elves she was expecting.

"For reference, these elves look more like Tolkien's elves. They are tall and thin, have pointy ears, and are immortal. They shift into human form when in the presence of humans," I said.

"Why?"

"It's a long story, and I promise we'll get back to it when we have more time," I replied. I put my hands around her waist and eased her to the right so we could look at the buildings around the town square.

"Santa's Village is like any other small town. There's a market, clothing store, shoe store, a dentist, and other professionals the townsfolk might need. It's where the elves have lived for millennia and where the pack and teachers live during the school year."

I pointed out all the buildings. We moved around the model until we were behind the school. "Over here are the stables. It's where we train in reindeer form and where Santa's sleigh is stored and maintained."

"But if the elves don't make toys, and there isn't a workshop, what does Santa deliver on Christmas night?" Kayla asked. She waved at the Village with one hand while the other rested on her cocked hip.

"Hope," I said, but as I took a breath to explain further, the lights blinked. "We must go back in. I'll explain later, I promise."

She crossed her arms and made a show of pouting, but I could tell she wasn't angry. She was curious, and I had piqued her interest.

"Come on. It's time for me to show off!" I said. I grabbed her hand, and we ran back to the ballroom.

13

KAYLA

When we entered the ballroom, the overhead lights were dimmed, and some spotlights were swirling around the room like we were in one of London's top nightclubs. Music was blaring through the speakers, the bass rattling my ribcage. Connor kissed my cheeks and left me with Spencer, Seraphina's boyfriend.

One by one, spots were lit down the middle of the room, and people parted like the Red Sea. Connor and the eleven other shifters took their place under each of the lights; Oliver was the first, and Connor the last. The music was replaced by what sounded like tribal drums. It shook the ground, and I swear I felt electricity run through my body. The air was crackling with it.

It's the magic.

Eyes trained on the twelve figures in front of me, I stared in astonishment as they shifted in unison. The gold shimmer spun around them, and, poof, they were reindeer. They marched in tandem, with military-like precision, with a one-two-hold movement that reminded me of show horses. They were definitely showing off.

They made their way onto the stage and lined up two by two like they might get ready to pull Santa's sleigh. They were still moving in time with the beat of the drum. People started clapping to the same rhythm, and the beat got faster. The excitement in the room was palpable.

Santa's coming.

I could feel it in my bones. I searched the stage, but I couldn't see him, nor a door he might arrive from. The first two reindeer started marching again, turning right this time, and the rest followed. They arced in a circle until they were behind the last two, and all the reindeer faced the circle's centre.

The drums stopped, and so did the clapping. The gold shimmer was back, thicker than it had been before. I could hear sleigh bells now, loud and reverberating throughout the room. Smoke started creeping along the floor and swirling around the reindeer's feet. There was a loud bang, sparkles everywhere, and there was Santa, surrounded by the twelve shifters, back in their human form.

Everyone erupted in cheers and applause. Santa and the shifters bowed in unison, and Oliver led the way down the centre aisle, the others following him until only Santa remained.

When Connor came to stand next to me, he was beaming.

"What did you think," he asked in a whisper near my ear as he slipped a hand in mine.

"You were amazing," I breathed. I turned to look at him and saw his eyes glowing. The other reindeer had the same green glow as I cast a glance around. I squeezed his hand; he squeezed back.

"What do you think of the big guy? Is he everything you imagined him to be?"

No, Santa wasn't at all how I imagined. I had expected a

rotund grandfatherly figure with a white beard and a gleam in his eye. The man standing on the stage, arms extended, taking in the applause, was no grandpa. I couldn't have guessed his age even if I had tried.

His pale smooth face glowed with youth, but his piercing black eyes held a distinct knowing that made you feel like he was older, wiser. He was tall, taller than even the tallest of the shifters, with a slim physique. The silver robes he wore glittered in the light and flowed as he moved.

He brought his hands together and bowed again, then gestured for us to sit. I had seen no chairs, but they were there. The applause died, and Santa removed his hood to reveal silver hair and very pointy ears.

"Santa's an elf?" I hissed at Connor.

"He's the elf King," he whispered.

When he spoke, I understood why elves shifted into human form. Instead of pearly white teeth, Santa had rows of razor-sharp ones, and his voice was high and lilting.

There was something ancient about him, something that whispered of power far older than the cheerful Christmas icon humans believed in. The way the other magical beings deferred to him wasn't just respect—it was reverence. I recalled stories my father had told me about the Elf Kingdoms of old, how their rulers had shaped the very forces of nature. Looking at Santa now, those stories suddenly seemed less like fairy tales and more like history.

"Welcome to our annual awards ceremony. I promise I won't bore you with a lengthy speech. Let's jump right into it," he began.

CONNOR

I could tell Santa freaked Kayla out by the way she squeezed my hand even harder when he started talking. When I had to leave her to accept my award for the Highest Performer at the Reindeer Games, I had to pry open her fingers and promise I'd be right back.

She kept a smile plastered on her face until the ceremony ended and they turned the lights back on. Buffet tables had appeared on either end of the room, and soft jazzy music was playing in the background.

Soon, the dancing would begin, and I hoped Kayla would be sufficiently recovered to do me the honour of a dance. I also knew Santa would mingle and would surely want to meet Kayla.

I searched the crowd for Sam and tried to make eye contact when I found her. When she finally saw me, I nodded in Kayla's direction and discretely pointed toward the ladies' washroom.

She said something to her friends and came our way.

"Quite the spectacle, wasn't it?" she said.

Kayla nodded, pensive. "I've never seen anything like it before."

"Fancy a trip to the loo, Kayla?"

"Yes!" replied Kayla, immediately launching herself in Sam's direction.

I mouthed 'thank you' to my sister and left Kayla in her capable hands. Sam had dealt with human guests to the Pole before; she'd know what to say. Hopefully, she'd get the colour back into Kayla's cheeks.

Meanwhile, though Seraphina and I weren't the best of mates, I quite liked Spencer. He might have a word of advice to share. I went over to where he was sitting and asked if I could join them.

"You're the star of the evening; how can we refuse," replied Seraphina. It was hard to tell if she was being sincere.

"Uh, thanks, I guess," I replied. After a pause, I turned to Spencer and asked, "How freaked out were you when you first saw Santa?"

He thought for a moment and replied, "Not very. Seraphina made me watch one of the Peter Pan movies, the one with the scary mermaid. You know the one?"

I nodded. "Well, she said that's what elves look like, and Santa was King of the elves," explained Spencer.

I scoffed. "Santa's nowhere near as frightening as those mermaids!"

"Right, but I'd braced myself for the worst."

I slapped my hand on my forehead. He was right, of course. "I'm such an idiot," I said.

"I can't say I disagree with you there," replied Seraphina with a sweet smile. "But don't be so hard on yourself. It's not like there's a manual on preparing outsiders for the realities of the North Pole. If she's a keeper, she'll rally. If not, just give her the forgetting potion and call it a lesson learned."

"I really hope she's a keeper," I said to no one in particular.

14
KAYLA

I was grateful to get away from the party. It was beautiful and magical, but I needed space to sort out my brain. This was all just too much for a girl from Oxford.

Samantha led me into the loo, where the music was thankfully muted. I was surprised to see that it wasn't like a regular loo. Instead, it was a fancy sitting room with red and green velvet chairs. A row of sinks was in front of a mirror on one side of the room.

"Where are the toilets?" I asked Sam.

Her eyes sparkled as she pointed at a large oak door at the back of the room. "Through there. There are two lines of stalls for us to do our business. The sitting area is separated if we just need a quiet place to relax or refresh our makeup."

"Oh, I should have collected my clutch," I groaned. After all that dancing, I probably needed to touch up my makeup.

"You look perfect," Sam told me.

She gestured for me to sit and got a damp towel to put on the back of my neck. The beautiful red dress that Crystal bought me shimmered under the twinkling lights. It looked like we were under a billion stars, each caught in a snowflake.

"How are you doing?" Sam asked me.

"It's overwhelming," I admitted to her. "It's all magnificent. But just a few weeks ago, I no longer believed in magic. I wanted to, but I didn't. Now I'm at the North Pole for New Year's!"

Sam laughed, then her face pinched with worry. "Does it change how you feel about Connor?"

I thought about the question. The reindeer shifter had drawn me in from the moment I met him. Just thinking about him made me smile. It calmed some of the panic that I felt in this situation.

"No," I told her. "It doesn't change how I feel at all. Connor is amazing. He's kind and funny. I love him."

Sam's grin grew even bigger. "You do?"

My cheeks warmed, but I grinned back. "Yeah. I do. That's the one magical thing that I never stopped believing in. I always believed in love at first sight. Although, in our case, it wasn't exactly first sight. Not until we got stuck in that elevator together."

Sam laughed with me. "I'm glad that it stopped working, then! You make him happy."

"I do?" I asked, not sure if I believed her.

"Would I lie to you?"

I smiled. No. No, she wouldn't. "I'm very grateful to be part of this world, Sam. Even if it's overwhelming right now. I never want to leave."

Every word was true. Saying it aloud helped me feel better about the whole situation. I just needed some time to understand things better.

"Oh, that reminds me. Is the pack leader the same as an alpha?" I asked her.

Sam nodded. "Mostly, yes. All reindeer shifters are part of the herd. Only the ones that pull Santa's sleigh are part of the pack. The pack leader is the one who runs the reindeer games and helps Santa choose who will lead the sleigh."

"Oh, so he doesn't lead it?" I asked.

"No. The pack leader leads the pack by caring for everyone and being aware of their strengths and weaknesses. It's a critical position." Sam sighs. "Connor hopes to be pack leader someday. I hope Santa can see his potential."

I thought about Santa with silver hair, a slender build, and sharp teeth. I shivered. "Santa scares me."

Sam laughed. "Only because you don't know him. And because you believed in that jolly nonsense most of your life. Come on, let's get back to the ball."

A jolly fat Santa had always seemed comforting to me. Still frowning, I followed her out of the loo.

As we got back to the party, Connor came over to me. He beamed, looking dashing in his green velvet suit. All my doubts were washed away.

"Do you want to dance?" he asked me.

"Yes," I said.

I took his hand, and we danced. As I gazed into his eyes, the surrounding magic hummed in time with the music.

I wish I could tell my family about everything that's happening here, I thought. I knew I couldn't, though. And I'd have to live with that.

CONNOR

The magic of the North Pole seemed even more magical while I was dancing with Kayla. The enchanting decorations seemed brighter and more glittery, while the ambience was terrific. We danced the night away, our conversation flowing with ease. Talking with her was so easy. It amazed me.

"I don't want the night to end," she told me eventually. Then she sighed. "But I guess it has to end soon, doesn't it? What time is it, anyway?"

I laughed softly. "Well, we're at the North Pole. The convergence of all time zones. Technically, we don't have time."

"But you said that the North Pole ran on London time," she said, looking confused.

I nodded and then explained. "It's a bit complicated. We do time things as far as London time goes, but we're also out of time. It's a magical thing. So, when you look at the clock, you can see what time it is in London. But time doesn't really change."

"But we must have been here for hours," she said.

"Are you tired?" I asked her with a twinkle in my eye.

Kayla's eyes widened. "Now that you mention it... no. I'm not tired at all. Even though we've been dancing all this time."

"It's the magic," I told her.

"That's amazing," she said, marvelling.

I enjoyed the wonderment on her beautiful face. Then she sucked her lower lip between her teeth. She looked hesitant, and the expression was so adorable I couldn't help but drop a kiss on her forehead.

"There's something I'm confused about," she said.

"Go ahead and ask." I nodded at her encouragingly.

"Well..." She drew out the word. "Earlier, when I asked if Santa delivers presents worldwide, you said he delivers hope. But I don't understand. How can he do that?"

I nodded. I was expecting something like this. So much of Santa had been complicated with other stories that it was hard to sort out.

"Santa never delivered presents to people," I explained to her. "You see, Christmas is right before the darkest time of the year and the coldest winter months in the Northern Hemisphere. So, Santa flies worldwide, delivering feelings of hope, peace, and joy to fortify everyone against the dark and cold."

"Oh. How?"

This was what I'd be learning at Shifter School. "I don't know exactly. It's part of the magic. Part of his agreement with the angels, I think."

"Angels?"

"You don't think the elves are the most powerful beings, do you?" I asked her with a wink.

Kayla blinked, then smiled. "I see. But you said it was for the Northern Hemisphere."

"Yeah. Santa goes all over the world on Christmas Eve, but it's not the only day he spreads hope. It just is the most powerful day," I told her. "Eighty-seven per cent of the world's population lives in the Northern Hemisphere."

Kayla thought hard, her nose wrinkling in concentration. "I guess it makes sense. But why Christmas Eve? Isn't the Winter Solstice on December 20 or 21?"

Now I was stumped. "I'll know more once I've taken the History of Christmas class, but I think the date changed when more people started celebrating Christmas instead of the Solstice."

Kayla's eyes lit up, and she beamed at me, sliding her hands down my lapels. "History of Christmas?" she asked, bouncing excitedly. "You'll have to tell me all about it!"

A warm feeling flooded me. We were still swaying to the music, but suddenly, it seemed far away, the sound filtering through a tunnel.

I became aware of my heartbeat, fast and furious. Kayla's face was glowing, the soft curls around her face bobbing in slow motion.

I took a deep breath. I had blurted it out before, but I wanted to say this with purpose. My hands dropped from her waist and settled on top of hers. I looked into her beautiful blue eyes and said, "I love you, Kayla."

Her cheeks went pink, but her smile widened. "I love you, too, Connor."

I placed my hands on either side of her face and kissed her. The room disappeared as we floated on a cloud under the midnight sky.

15
KAYLA

We kissed for eons. Out of breath, we rested our foreheads together, hands clasped between us. This is what people meant when they said a kiss could stop time. Yes, this was pure magic.

My eyes fluttered open when I felt something cold settle on my cheek. Snowflakes! I lifted my face and saw a small cloud had settled over us on the dance floor. I giggled and looked back at Connor, whose face was beet red.

"That's what they do when things heat up on the dance floor. It's never happened to me before," he said.

I glanced at the other dancers. Most were ignoring the cloud, but a few of the younger couples were grinning and sending winks our way. My cheeks pinked, and I smiled sheepishly at Connor.

We resumed dancing, and I told Connor how much I loved snow and wished there was more of it in Oxford.

"Once, I even thought of moving to Canada," I said, and Connor laughed.

Someone cleared their throat behind me. Connor had turned serious, and I turned to see Santa. He was smiling, but his mouth was closed, so I couldn't see his teeth.

"I'm sorry, sir. I guess we got swept up in the heat of the moment, so to speak," hurried Connor.

"It's alright, Connor. I was coming over to ask if I could cut in," Santa asked. His gaze turned toward me, his eyes crinkling up at the edges.

It wasn't enough to quell the nerves that churned in my stomach.

"Kayla, may I have a dance?" Santa asked, hand outstretched.

I glanced at Connor, who smiled at me and nodded encouragingly. I swallowed nervously. "Ok-kay," I stammered.

Santa took my hand and led me to the centre of the ballroom. The crowd parted, and a waltz began. I was about to tell him I didn't know how to waltz when Santa swept me away. Magic or not, he was clearly better at this than Connor.

"I know I look intimidating," Santa said as we danced. "I can shift into human form if you would prefer."

As I stared at his face, I realized I didn't want him to. Yes, I was intimidated by his features, but why should I be? This was Santa Claus. I wrote him so many letters growing up. I took a deep breath and shook my head.

"No, please don't. I need to get used to the magic."

"I'm glad. It shows that you're willing to change your mindset for Connor's sake," Santa said.

He asked me questions about my family, and we talked for some time. I was eager to tell him about them all. My heart felt oddly heavy by the time I was done.

"I wish I could bring them here," I blurted before I could lose my nerve.

Santa raised an eyebrow at me. "Do you?"

"Yes. I know the Oath means I can tell them the truth, and their minds will change whatever I say so that we can understand each other. It means it's not really a full lie," I said, my brows furrowing. "And I'm very grateful for that, of course. I understand why it's needed. You don't know my family."

"True," Santa said. "I'm not omniscient."

I sighed, thinking about how excited everyone would be if they could see all of this. "I guess I don't like the idea of the half-lies that the Oath would change it to. I don't enjoy keeping them in the dark about what's happening in my life. And I wish I could share the magic with them. It's been a hard year."

"I know, dear. It's been difficult all over the world these last few years. But you must have hope."

I smiled at him. It was amazing how easily he'd put me at ease. "I will. And I'll follow all the rules, I promise."

"Good. But there is something you should know." Santa stopped dancing and looked at me seriously. The music had stopped, and he was leading me to where Connor sat with his friends.

"There's a potion you can drink to erase your memories of the North Pole."

I gaped at him and dropped his hand. "Why would I want to do that?"

"If you feel you cannot live a lie... or if the Oath fails," he said, his expression serious. "The option is available."

A shiver ran down my spine. Forget everything? I would cherish these moments forever. But I understood his point. Would it be too much to never tell my family and friends about the North Pole? About Connor?

CONNOR

Kayla seemed distracted after her dance with Santa. We danced and talked, but she seemed guarded and tense.

"Are you okay?" I asked her when we headed home.

"I'm just thinking about my family," she told me, then smiled reassuringly. "I'll figure it out. Don't worry."

When we arrived back home, Sam showed Kayla to the guest room. I went to my bedroom and changed into my pyjamas. Even though it had been a grand party and I was tired, my brain was too busy to sleep.

I kept thinking about what my friends said, wondering if Kayla was a 'keeper.' I loved her and wanted to see what the future would look like together... but what if she didn't feel the same way?

What if the magic was just too much for her? Could that be why she got distant after her dance with Santa?

I groaned as I tossed and turned. No matter how comfortable I was, I couldn't get to sleep. I had too many thoughts in my head.

Eventually, I realized I would not get to sleep at all.

I threw off my blankets, put on a dressing gown, and padded to the kitchen for a midnight snack. Maybe if I had some warm milk and a biscuit, it would put me to sleep.

As I approached, I was surprised to see that the light was on. I entered the kitchen and grinned when I saw Kayla. She stood in the middle of the kitchen, looking around with a confused expression on her face.

She was just too cute! I burst out in laughter.

Kayla jumped and turned to me. "Oh, Connor! You scared me."

"I'm sorry," I said. I walked over, wrapped her in a side hug, and kissed the top of her head. "If you could see your expression, you would have laughed too."

This time, she laughed with me. "I was that funny, huh?"

"Yeah, you were."

Kayla gestured around the kitchen. "Your parents told me I could have whatever I wanted, but I don't know where anything is."

"Hmm. What do you want?"

"I was thinking maybe some popcorn," she replied. "I can't sleep and thought I'd like to watch a movie."

My eyes lit up. That was a great idea! We made a big bowl and headed to the living room.

"Won't we disturb your family?" she asked.

"No, this house has thick walls. No one will hear a thing."

I snuggled next to her and selected a Christmas classic.

"I love Christmas movies," Kayla said. "They're my favourite."

"Mine, too."

This was exactly how I imagined dating would be. Huddled under a blanket, watching movies and munching on popcorn. I mean, the kissing had been nice, and I couldn't wait to do it again, but this was lovely.

We must have fallen asleep because I woke to Sam shaking me

the following day. My arm was wrapped around Kayla, the other still holding the empty popcorn bowl.

We made flapjacks for breakfast, and Kayla was bright and animated as she talked with my parents. They asked about her family, her friends, and her plans for school next year. I couldn't help feeling like she belonged.

All too soon, though, Kayla's cousin came to pick her up. I walked her to the car and kissed her softly. "I'll call you," I promised.

"You better," she said, jabbing a finger against my chest. She slipped into the car and waved as it drove away.

16

KAYLA

As expected, Crystal asked me a million questions about what happened. I kept telling her she had to wait until we got home so I could tell everyone at the same time. My whole body felt warm and glowing, like I was coming to the end of a great Christmas movie.

The end.

The happiness dimmed a little. This wasn't the end of my movie, was it? Connor and I were just at the beginning! I wondered what happened next. All holiday romance films end with the first kiss...

I guess I'll have to wait and see.

I smiled to myself and walked into the house. My head was still full of the magic of the North Pole. Everything remained vivid and clear. I had been afraid last night that I'd wake up today and find it was all a dream.

But it wasn't. No dream was as tangible as my memories of the North Pole were.

"We're home," Crystal called.

A herd of family members greeted us. They asked questions all over each other. I had to laugh and waved my hands to make them stop.

"Tell us everything," Mum demanded when we entered the living room.

"Where to start?" I wondered out loud. "Well, I guess first you should know that Connor and his family are reindeer shifters. They can turn into reindeer and pull Santa's sleigh."

Mum's eyes widened, and her jaw dropped.

I wondered what the Oath was translating to them. I continued describing going to the North Pole and everything that happened there. When I got to the part where I danced with Santa, my brother Andy laughed.

"What's so funny?" I asked him.

"You danced with Santa Claus? Wasn't Mrs. Claus jealous?" he giggled.

I opened my mouth to retort, but nothing came out. My parents, aunts, uncles, and cousins were all staring at me with confused expressions. A few of them looked like they thought I might be going insane.

An icy finger crept up my spine. The Oath was supposed to mask my words. They shouldn't have heard anything about the North Pole and Santa.

"Um..." I swallowed hard. "When we came home, I couldn't sleep. So I went to the kitchen, and Connor came, too. We made popcorn and sat watching films until we both fell asleep. That's everything."

Dad tugged at his ear. "You mean you went to somewhere decorated as the North Pole, right?"

My breath caught in my throat. He wasn't supposed to have heard that!

"What's going on?" I wondered out loud.

"And you danced with someone dressed like Santa," Mum probed.

Aunt Mathilda asked, "Did you feel odd being the only one without a costume?"

I looked between them. My hands grew cold. Did I do something wrong? Maybe I had drunk a bad batch of the Oath potion. Or perhaps I shouldn't have had so many delicious fizzy drinks while at the party.

"You're not supposed to have understood me," I said, panicking. "You were supposed to have thought I went to some ambassadorial ball or something! But you... you heard everything, didn't you?"

Crystal propped her elbows on the table. "If you mean that you just told us you went to the North Pole with a reindeer shifter who led Santa's sleigh this year, then yeah."

I rubbed my hands against my trousers. "And... and you believe me?" I asked, hoping that they'd all burst into laughter like Andy.

Their faces answered it all.

They believed me.

"You've never been someone who just made things up," Mum said. "Even when you were playing games about magic, it always seemed... well, real to you."

I gulped. My heart pounded. The Oath hadn't worked. I had just spilt the tea about everything.

Would Connor get into trouble because of me? Would Santa erase our memories?

CONNOR

My family always spent New Year's Day with elderly shifters. Though they didn't recognize us and could no longer shift, we still brought along blankets, hot tea, and minced pies. It was the singing that led the odd Shifter to take human form, and they were always happy to see a friendly face when it happened.

I came home to a panicked message from Kayla, and my cheerful mood evaporated. She had been vague on the details, saying only that I should ring her back immediately.

I swallowed the lump in my throat and rang her.

"Hey, Kayla. What's going on?"

"The Oath failed. I told my family everything - aunts, cousins, the whole lot, and they heard every word," she told me. She spoke rapidly, explaining to me what had happened.

She was in quite a state. I tried calming her down, but it was infectious. I'd never heard of the Oath failing like this. Something must have gone wrong, but what? Dad got the Oath from the elves himself just before Kayla got to the house yesterday.

The Oath was one of the oldest forms of bonding magic in our world, dating back to when the seasonal courts first established balance. It was supposed to be unbreakable—a mixture of elemental magic and ancient promises that redirected human perception rather than altering memory. If it had failed, there was something truly unusual about Kayla and her family.

"I'll talk to my family. I'm sure we can figure it out," I said, hoping I was right. "Don't worry. There's got to be a simple way to fix this."

I hung up and faced my parents and sister. They all watched me with concern in their eyes.

"What's wrong?" Mum asked.

"It's Kayla. The Oath didn't take. She told her entire family everything about the North Pole, and now they know," I said. I chewed my lip as worry ate at my stomach. "Are we in trouble?"

Dad stood. "Of course not, Connor. Call Kayla back and tell her to bring her family here. We'll take them to Santa. He'll know what to do."

I nodded. "Okay, that's a good plan," I said as I texted Kayla to get over here ASAP. Her reply was instant.

> On our way. xo

I need to calm down for Kayla's sake.

Mum got busy tidying up the house, and Sam put out a plate of biscuits as Dad brewed some tea.

"It's going to be okay, Connor," Sam told me as the cars pulled into the driveway. "Santa will understand this isn't your fault."

I nodded dully. I wasn't really worried about myself, more about what this meant for Kayla.

I knew it would affect my family if Santa decided I did something wrong. The Prancer family was still regaining their reputation. But I just couldn't worry about myself. The worst possible thing that could happen was that Santa decided that all of Kayla's family would have to forget.

Kayla would also forget about me... or have to give up contact with her family, which I knew she would never do.

My heart ached just thinking about her having to choose.

Her family looked awed and nervous as Mum and Dad welcomed them into the house. We couldn't all fit into the fireplace to get to the North Pole, so we took it a few at a time. Mum sent me through first with Kayla and her parents.

Kayla laced her fingers through mine as we stepped into the ballroom. The decorations from last night had been taken down, leaving vaulted ceilings and a wide, open floor.

"This is so beautiful," her mum whispered.

Soon, everyone was here. They all looked around with awed expressions. I swallowed nervously, then sighed. There wasn't any point in being nervous, was there? We had followed the protocol to a T.

"Let's have a seat and wait for Santa. I called his assistant, and he should be joining us presently," Dad said as he motioned to the lounging area.

"What will happen when he arrives?" asked Kayla's dad.

"I assume he'll have a potion for you to drink to make you forget what Kayla told you."

Kayla squeezed my hand tightly. Looking into her eyes, I saw the same fear that curled in my stomach.

I didn't want what might be our last moments together to be ruined by fear. Kayla's family members were whispering amongst themselves, worried expressions all around.

"Since you're going to forget anyway, perhaps I could give you a tour of the village. Any takers?" I suggested.

Kayla sighed with relief. "That would be wonderful!"

17
KAYLA

All of my fears drained away as Connor took us outside. Everything was covered in a glittering blanket of snow. There were dozens of buildings in Santa's village. Each one was unique and painted in bright, captivating colours.

"There's snow everywhere, but it's not cold," Crystal said, shaking her head in amazement.

I smiled at her. "Did you forget what I said about magic?"

Crystal rolled her eyes and stuck her tongue out at me. Even though she was a big-shot lawyer, she still acted very immature sometimes.

"It's exactly what I thought it would be like," Mum said. She giggled and broke into a run, pulling Dad with her.

I laughed out loud in surprise as they dove into a pile of snow. There, they started making snow angels. I shook my head at them and turned to find all of my family were playing. Andy and Crystal threw perfectly formed snowballs at each other, laughing in delight. My aunts and uncles were piling snow together, and my cousins were already making snowmen.

Connor wrapped his arm around me. "Wow. They're taking all of this way better than I expected."

I sighed happily, leaning into him. This was just as magical as it had been during the ball. Maybe even more so because this was my family. I could see how happy they were. Seeing how the magic was making them all act like kids again made me smile.

"You know," I whispered to him, "I think I'm not the only one in my family still believing in magic. Maybe that's why the Oath didn't work. Because even if they were all dealing with adult stuff, they remained innocent at heart?"

Connor kissed my temple. "It looks like it."

But unfortunately, even seeing my family so happy couldn't bolster me against my fears for long. My smile slipped away as I turned to him. I held Connor's hands tightly as I looked into his eyes.

"No matter what happens, I will always love you," I told him seriously. "I wouldn't trade away the time we've spent together for anything. No matter what Santa decides, I love you."

Connor blinked rapidly like he was trying not to cry. "I love you, too."

His warm hands cupped my cheeks. Then he kissed me. Our lips pressed together, and the tingle of magic swept through me. I closed my eyes, leaning into the kiss. This might be our last time together. I wanted to make it count.

"Uh, oh, PDA alert," called a voice behind us.

Connor and I broke apart. We turned to find Crystal and Sam heading toward us. They walked arm-in-arm, best friends already. Both watched us with a teasing twinkle in their eyes. My face heated, but I only shook my head.

"You're making it weird," Connor complained.

Sam and Crystal glanced at each other, then burst out laughing.

Connor's dad came up behind them. He called for us all to gather. "Santa has arrived," he said.

My throat felt like the Sahara Desert. I swallowed hard as I clutched Connor's hand. We looked at each other. A fierce determination burned in his eyes. It made me feel better, but I hoped he wouldn't do anything that would get him into trouble.

"We should go," he said.

I nodded.

We headed back to the ballroom. My family talked and laughed. I wished I could join in, but my stomach twisted into too many knots. I desperately hoped I could keep the magic. I didn't want to give it up. I didn't want to give up Connor.

But I would do whatever Santa asked me to if it meant keeping Connor safe.

CONNOR

My heart pounded as we entered the ballroom. Santa was waiting for us, wearing his human disguise, thank the stars. Gone were the pointed ears and the razor-blade teeth. While he was neither fat nor jolly, he wasn't quite so menacing either.

"Whoa," Crystal whispered to Sam. "Santa's hot!"

Sam shushed her. I winced. Didn't Crystal realize what a dire situation this was? But then, I guessed she wouldn't. After all, she hadn't known that Santa was real until that morning.

"Hello, everyone," Santa greeted, opening his arms. It was like a hug; I know I felt better right away.

That was the thing about Santa. How could someone who worked tirelessly to bring hope to the world be someone you'd be afraid of? I trusted him to make the right choices here. Even if I was worried about what the right thing might be. He wouldn't let us down.

"Hello," murmured various members of Kayla's family.

Crystal put her hands on her hips. "So, where's Mrs. Claus? And why doesn't she have a name?"

Kayla groaned, closing her eyes.

But Santa only chuckled at Crystal's boldness. "My wife is busy with her work," he told her. "And she does have a name. She has many names. You probably know her as Easter or Mother Earth."

Crystal's jaw dropped. She didn't seem to know what to say in response to that.

Santa smiled kindly at her, then turned to Kayla. "So, what seems to be the problem?"

"Well..." Kayla took a deep breath.

She told Santa everything. She got flustered a few times, but Santa listened patiently. He nodded and praised her quick thinking in calling me when she realized the Oath hadn't worked.

Once she was done, he patted her shoulder. "You did everything right, Kayla. Thank you."

She nodded, letting out a relieved sigh.

"Now, as for the rest of you," Santa said as he turned to her family, "I will give you a choice. You can either take the Oath yourselves and remember everything or take a potion to make you forget. It will seem like a pleasant dream you can't quite remember."

I straightened.

"We get to choose?" Kayla's mum asked.

Santa chuckled. "Of course! The Oath never fails."

My jaw hung slack. "What?"

Santa's eyes twinkled in mischief. "You see, while I was dancing with Kayla last night, I undid the Oath. It was rather sneaky of me, I'll admit. But how she talked about her family made me realize how much she loved them. And I can easily see the love that you two share."

He smiled warmly at us.

Kayla and I both blushed, but I grinned, pleased.

"It seemed unbearably selfish of me to ask Kayla to lie to her family," Santa said.

"I was worried about that," Kayla admitted.

"It's cumbersome, knowing that there's a part of your life that you can't share with the people you love," Santa said. "Which is why now you all have a choice."

Crystal cheered, throwing her hands into the air. "I'll take the Oath! I'm a lawyer; I'm good at keeping secrets!"

Everyone laughed. Kayla's immediate family members enthusiastically agreed to take the Oath, while a few of her aunts and uncles requested the forgetting potion.

Santa snapped his fingers, and two trays appeared on a nearby table.

"The red potion is the forgetting potion," Santa said and pointed to the fireplace we'd come through. "Take it with you and wait until just before entering your car to take it."

The aunts and uncles said goodbye and left with their potions.

The rest of Kayla's family reached for the green vials. Santa led us to a new fireplace. His eyes twinkled as he laid his hand on the hearth.

"This will be your gateway to get to and from the North Pole," he told them. "You're welcome to stop by whenever you want to. We recruit new helpers year-round."

He winked, and everyone laughed.

"As for you," he said, looking at me.

I gulped.

He smiled. "You've chosen well, Connor. Kayla is definitely a keeper."

Relief washed over me. Kayla and I turned to each other. We were both grinning like idiots. I didn't care that everyone was watching. I had to kiss her; it was the best day of my life.

The End.

Did you enjoy *Holiday Shifters*?

Please consider leaving a review on Goodreads, Bookbub, or your favorite retailer.

Reviews help me reach new readers.

Read **Freshman Frost**, the next book in the **North Pole University** series.

Have you read **Oath Keeper**?

This FREE North Pole University story is set between **Holiday Shifters** and **Freshman Frost**

ABOUT THE AUTHOR

Positive, uplifting books and stories.

Marie-Hélène Lebeault is a Canadian speculative fiction author whose work spans over fifty books, a dozen anthologies and countless short stories. Her short fiction, published in venues including *Dreamforge, Dirty Magick, Chortle, Quest,* and *Protocolized,* dwells on identity, memory, and the quiet shifts that reshape a life. She enjoys wandering new landscapes, both real and imagined, always searching for the stories tucked between the cracks. Find her at www.mhlebeault.com.

Follow on Social Media, she'd love to hear from you!

facebook.com/mhlebeaultauthor

x.com/mhlebeault

instagram.com/mhlebeault

amazon.com/author/mhlebeault

bookbub.com/authors/marie-helene-lebeault

goodreads.com/mhlebeault

linkedin.com/in/mhlebeault

tiktok.com/@mhlebeaultauthor

ALSO BY THE AUTHOR

Defenders of the Realm - YA Epic Fantasy

A Journey to Power

The Quest for the Emerald Rattleback

A Summer of Discovery

The Quest for the Sacred Tree

A Summer of Opposites

The Quest for the Phantom Feather

A Summer of Courage

The Quest for the Kraken's Ink

A Summer of Destiny

The Quest for the Cursed Mirrors

A Summer of Unity

The Battle of the Blossoming Flame (FREE)

Defenders of the Realm - Special Edition Hardcover Set

The Evers Series - YA Science Fantasy

The Traveler's Handbook (FREE)

The Ancestors' Key

The Academy

The Time Walker

The World Jumper

5th Anniversary Deluxe Edition Omnibus

The Lost Key

Blood Magick Trilogy - YA Urban Fantasy

The Blood Mage

Blood Magick

Blood Legacy

Bonus Epilogue (FREE)

Deluxe Extended Edition Omnibus

Standalones

Clarity Castle

What Happens Next?

Ghost Stories

Echoes of Tomorrow

Utopia

The Tidepost Chronicles - Middle Grade Fantasy

The Tide Runners

The Drowned City

The Sky-Reef Chase

The Silent Tide

The Living Current

Picture Books

Fairy Grandmother: Millie Goes to Antarctica

Fairy Grandmother: Millie Goes to the North Pole

Fairy Grandmother: Millie Goes to China

Fairy Grandmother: Millie Goes to Africa

(Also available in French, Spanish, German, and Italian)